Destiny's Children: Joby

By: Catherine Hagedorn

CHAPTER ONE

MEETINGS

My story starts on the day I was born. I do not know everything about my beginnings, and I doubt I ever will. What I do know is that I was found hidden among bushes by the oldest woman of our tribe. I was sleeping soundly and had been bundled carefully to keep me warm, a sure sign that I hadn't been abandoned and that whoever had left me planned on coming back. At the sound of her approach, I woke up and began to cry. She sat with me and soothed me, believing that my mother would return for me, wherever she had gone.

The story I had been told was as she sat and waited, a group of men being led by the King of the North passed by on horseback. She said that the king had a crazy look in his eyes. She didn't know for sure who he was pursuing, but instinct told her to shrink down into the bushes and keep me as quiet as she possibly could.

Still, she stayed there with me after the men had passed by. She waited for what she assumed was two hours, and then the men came back around with a woman captive. The king had the woman seated in front of him on his horse. He had her tied there. It seemed unnecessary because she looked so tired and defeated, as if she had been through hell. Even with the restraints and the look of defeat he held her tightly. Though she was obviously his captive, there was a sort of softness in the way he kept her with him. As the wise old woman watched them intently, the young lady looked in the direction of the bushes and caught the old woman's eyes peering at her.

"Please," she said to the king softly, "let me go into those bushes so that I can go to the bathroom. I promise that I won't run away. I have no reason to run anymore anyway. I just need a moment of peace and one last moment of freedom before you imprison me forever."

"You should not have run," the king argued, but he untied her and let her down and the woman made her way to the bushes, where I was hidden with the old woman.

By this time it was clear to the old woman that this was my mother, and as she approached the bushes and tears began to fill her eyes, the old woman felt a sense of compassion for her. She didn't seem like any particular danger, and through past experience the old woman knew that this girl (and she was only a girl of about twenty-one) was just another victim of the way that things had become.

Grandmother (as I would later come to call the old woman, just as every child in the tribe called her) moved back to make room for my mother as she came into the bushes. My mother slouched down so that her whole body would be hidden from the group of men not far from the bushes. She held out her arms for me and Grandmother handed me to her, expecting that my mother's distress was brought on by the realization that she would soon have to reveal me to the men and was anxious about my safety.

"Count," the king yelled from the trail, "I want to know you are not making an attempt to escape. I need to know that you are not trying to slip out of those bushes."

And my mother counted. Each number was choked out in a fury of sobs, and Grandmother knew at that moment, that I wouldn't be going with her. She held me for only a few mere moments and then she handed me back to Grandmother. Before she left, she took the necklace around her neck and handed it to Grandmother. It was gold with a long chain and was molded into the figure of a lion. The lion had a small green jewel for an eye.

"This is so that in the future, people will know who she is, and where she belongs," my mother sobbed, "do not let her lose it, and do not let her wear it until you are absolutely sure that there will be no harm in her doing so. Tell her that it is a gift from her mother, but nobody can know that she is my daughter. She is in more danger than you could possibly know." Grandmother nodded her agreement.

"Are you still in there?" My mother had stopped counting to give this important message to Grandmother, and the king had gotten suspicious. He had dismounted his horse, and my mother hurried out of the bushes before he could make his way into them.

"I'm sorry," she apologized, "I was just distracted for a moment and forgot to count."

"Where is your necklace?" he demanded. My mother reached up toward her naked neck and gasped in astonishment.

"I must have dropped it along the way somewhere. I was not very concerned with my belongings as I was trying to save my son's life."

The king seemed to accept that statement as the truth. Grandmother found out later that there was a boy that my mother had brought into the next town to be cared for, but he could not be saved.

As soon as they were out of sight Grandmother picked me and all of her belongings up and headed for the town that my mother and the men had just come from. She carefully hid the lion necklace in her pocket and tucked it so far in that there was no chance of it falling out or being accidently discovered. In addition to it being dangerous to be found with me, it would also be an interesting topic of discussion for anyone around as to how an old tribeswoman from the forests came into contact with any little bit of gold. The tribes have always been disinterested in that sort of thing, and never carried anything on them that they wouldn't need to live.

Grandmother stopped at the first house that she came to in the little town and knocked on the door, hoping that the people inside would be kind and offer her a hand. It had been years since she cared for a baby and, of course, she had no milk or clothing for me. She was in luck. The door opened and a sweet, middle-aged woman opened the door.

"Well," the woman smiled, sadly, "it's good to see a healthy baby come into our lives today. We have a poor little darling being buried in the cemetery right as we speak. He died not long ago, and then the king came and took away his mother. Poor thing was a slave. She tried to escape to freedom with her unborn child and ended up in labor along the way. Well then, what's this one's story? I know she isn't yours."

"My great grand-daughter," Grandmother lied as convincingly as she could, "she took sick along the trail back home. She died an hour after childbirth. This one here looks strong enough, but I have nothing for her. It was a while before my grand-daughter was supposed to have her. I was hoping you could spare something to get the baby's strength up so I can take her home to her father."

"I will do what I can," the middle-aged woman said. An hour later, Grandmother had enough supplies for me to take me back to the tribe with her.

She took me to a single woman in the tribe named Sheena. Sheena was young and beautiful, but hardheaded and independent. She had little time for anybody, and least of all, an infant. She had been the outcast of the tribe for as long as anybody could remember, although she contributed more than any other person. She was just not friendly like everyone else.

"Why would you bring this baby to me?" Sheena argued with Grandmother. "I cannot take care of this baby. I am too busy. I have too much to do. I will not love it."

"Everyone in this tribe has their job to do, Sheena," Grandmother smiled. "This job is yours now. I am the oldest and I make the rules. You have been alone for too long. Now it is time for you to learn how to contribute socially. You will be responsible for making sure this child is brought up right."

"You know I can't do that," Sheena roared. "I do not know how to be social with anybody. Why can't you take care of her? You were the one who brought her here. She isn't even one of us. Why does she need to learn to live like us? Drop her off with town people."

"I am too old to take care of any more children. My time in this world is coming to an end. I can't die happily if I know that I am leaving somebody behind who depends on me for so much. She needs to be hidden. The forest is the best place for her to be so, and I know that she will be very important to us all one day. You are also the best person to care for her. You can teach her how to be independent, and how to fight. If I am right about this child, she is going to need to know how to do both. You cannot fail her in that. Besides, I only got a quick glimpse of her mother, but you look very much like her. As this child grows, she may take on that look, and it will be good for us all if she is being raised by someone who could possibly pass for her mother. It is as much for our safety as it is for hers. Finally, she might do you some good. You play it off as much as you want that you are happy being alone, but I can tell there are times when it is a burden, even for you. I've been watching you, Sheena, and I know that you are lonely. Don't try to fool me, I'm very old. I know how to read people. And as for her not being one of us, I seem to remember finding you alone in the forest once, too."

Sheena could not argue with Grandmother, she was right. For about a year, she had been feeling the weight of her independence, but no matter how hard she tried she couldn't swallow her pride enough to let people know that she was open for company. The most interaction she had with any of the other people in the tribe came only when she had brought in a fresh kill from a hunt, or something that she had foraged. The tribe would thank her, and then turn away, because they knew she would not want to be bothered with any other conversation. Sheena would retire to her caravan and brood over how she just could not seem to make people take an interest in her. She didn't know it yet, but all that was going to change.

So Sheena took me in. She says that the first night was the hardest of her life. She never paid much attention to babies in her life, although she had plenty of opportunities, being brought up as the oldest of twelve children. When I cried it made her crazy, but instead of being able to just escape as she had done when she was younger, she was the one who had to figure out what was wrong with me and make me stop. She says that even though it was horrendous the feeling of accomplishment she got when she finally got the hang of it was better than any feeling she had ever had in her life.

The next morning, a couple came to Sheena's caravan. They had already had six children, and they wanted to take me. They told Sheena they knew she wasn't equipped to handle me. They said it would be a relief when they took me off her hands. Sheena took one look at them and told them that I wasn't a burden and that they should be ashamed of talking about a baby like that, especially about her baby. It was in that moment that Sheena knew that she loved me, and that she felt a deep connection with me that she couldn't explain. It was that night that Sheena stopped looking like a hermit to the rest of the tribe. In the years to come, Sheena became one of the most well liked members of the tribe, as well as one of the most productive.

The night after the couple came, Sheena was rocking me back and forth in a comfortable little rocking chair she had made and was singing me to sleep. She was looking in my steadily drooping eyes when she realized something that horrified her. She had been with me for three days, and I still didn't have a name.

"Oh, baby," Sheena whispered, "I'm so sorry that I didn't think of something to call you. I've never done this before, forgive me. You've had so many afflictions in your short life already. You've been abandoned, and there is a threat of danger that will always be around for you, and who knows what would have happened to you if Grandmother had not found you. How could I have added not naming you to that list? There is nothing else to call you, but Joby."

And as my eyelids closed shut, she placed me in the little wooden box that had been made temporarily for my bed and then made her way to the dresser. She pulled out that little chain with the lion with the green eye and pondered it for a moment or two. She says that she thought about throwing that necklace so far into the forest that nobody would ever find it again, and it could pose no danger to me, but she changed her mind knowing that it could hold the answer to my destiny.

"How could this little trinket be so important and so dangerous to you at the same time?" Sheena asked the sleeping infant that stole her heart in a matter of hours. It would be many years before any of us would know the answer to that.

CHAPTER TWO

THE WAY THINGS ARE

"Joby!" Sheena was screaming at me again from the clearing in the forest, where all of the caravans were sitting. "Joby, you better get your butt home before I come in there and get you. And if I have to find you, you are going to be in real trouble!"

"You better go, Joby," my best friend, River, teased, "Your mommy is calling you."

"I'm not afraid of her!" I spit back, climbing higher in the tree we were in. "She's not my mother anyway. I don't have to listen to her."

It had been eight years and Sheena had accidently let it slip the morning before that she was not really my mother. I had taken it badly and decided that instead of accepting the fact that I had been adopted by her, I was going to challenge her authority.

"Okay," River stammered, taken aback by my statement, "but I am afraid of her. And if she finds you, she's going to find me. Then we will both be in trouble. Please, just go home."

"I don't want to," I stated firmly, "I'm going to find my real mother."

River looked at me, pleading with his eyes. Then he began to climb down the tree. I knew Sheena could not see me in the trees, so it came as a shock to me when River ran up to her and pointed me out. I fumed. I would make sure to beat him up good that night.

"Chicken!" I screamed at him. "Tattle tail!"

"Get down here now!" Sheena scolded at me. "Or I will come up and get you."

I knew at this point that it would be a mistake for me not to come down and face her. I shot River a dirty look as my feet touched the ground, and he ran away back to the clearing. He knew what was coming to him.

"I've been yelling at you for half an hour and you didn't answer me. I know you could hear me from those trees. What were you thinking?" Sheena began to lecture. "You know when I start yelling at you it's probably for a good reason."

"I was looking for my real mother," I shot back. I wished that I wouldn't have the moment I saw her face. She looked a little hurt. I never saw Sheena look that hurt before.

"I'm sorry," I whispered.

"Never mind," Sheena sighed, "the caravan is moving again."

"Why?" I asked, upset. "We've only been here for two days, the last spot we only stayed at for four days. Why are we moving so much? I might be eight, but I'm not stupid. Something is going on. We usually stay at places for a month or more before we move on."

"I can't tell you yet," Sheena said, apologetically, "I want to, but I can't. You are too young, and I need you to just listen to me. I know you too well to know that if I tell you what is happening, you are going to go looking for trouble."

"I won't," I pleaded, "I promise."

"If you have anything that isn't already in the caravan," Sheena said forcefully, "you better go get it now. We will be leaving within an hour. We are going deeper within the forest. I think we might be making a new clearing."

The tribe rarely made a new clearing. In the eight years that I had been in the tribe, I had only seen it done one other time when I was five. The tribes in the forest had many clearings and would share them, as we were all nomadic. When a new tribe would come upon a clearing, they would fix it up and it would be left a little neater for the next tribe than if the tribes never shared. This kept every tribe in peace with each other. If a clearing was already inhabited, the two tribes would come together for a short period and share stories and secrets before one of the tribes decided to move on. Sometimes there would be a marriage between two members of different tribes, so it created a beneficial social environment as well. To make a new clearing that the other tribes didn't know about was exciting and a little bit rebellious, because the point of a clearing was so that everyone could use it if they needed it.

By the time we had been on the trail for a while, I knew something was definitely going on, and I got the strange feeling that it had something to do with me. The grown-ups were constantly saying things to each other, whispering so that the children couldn't hear them. Every once in a while I would look up to see an adult staring at me with a look of alarm on their face. They would quickly look away and pretend they were too busy with the moving to notice me. Throughout the move, people would inexplicably come up next to me and ask me how I was doing, and if I needed anything. It was as if they were all trying to keep an extremely close eye on me. I blamed Sheena. I thought that she might have said something to the tribe about me running off and not answering her.

By the third night of trudging deeper and deeper into the woods, we all got a shock. There was a new clearing. But there was something off about this one. It wasn't fully finished. That meant that the tribe that started it, couldn't have lived there for more than two days before moving on. It didn't even seem worth it to start a project and then to leave it right away. Something made the tribe leave.

"We can't go this way anymore," Grandmother shouted above all of the whispering voices. "It's obvious that going deeper into the forest isn't going to help us."

"Well, then where do we go?" Someone called out. "The children are tired, and frankly so are we."

"We'll stay here for the night." Grandmother said. "If this place was already hit, we should be safe for at least the night."

That night, as I was sleeping inside the caravan, I was awoken by the sound of Grandmother and Sheena talking in hushed voices outside. I slipped quietly out of my bed and crept to the door so that I could hear what they were saying.

"Grandmother," Sheena pleaded, "we need to send Joby away somewhere. It's becoming too dangerous for her here now. I don't think that we can protect her here anymore. We can go into town and see if we can find someone to take her in. She can do chores to earn her keep until this all blows over. Then we can bring her back."

"And would you want to be sent away from the forest when it is the only thing you have ever known?" Grandmother argued furiously.

"Besides, how are we going to send her away without her knowing why she is being sent away in the first place? That is something we both agree that we cannot tell her yet. And if something were to happen to the tribe? She will probably lose her necklace if we keep it with us, and she might be found easily if we tell her about it and send it with her. She will either lose her identity or lose her freedom. No, I think that the only thing left to do for her now is to keep her here and teach her to fight."

"She's not ready for that yet," Sheena disagreed. "I thought that we agreed that I would teach her fighting skills and how to use weapons when she was sixteen. She couldn't even hold a bow and arrow right at this age."

"She is remarkable, just like you were at that age." Grandmother smiled. "She will do wonderfully if you just give her the chance. You protect her too much. It is time for her to learn how to protect herself."

"I am ready," I blurted out. Grandmother and Sheena stopped talking.

"How long have you been listening to us?" Sheena scolded and motioned for me to come out of the caravan.

"I heard you talking and I woke up. I would rather be taught to fight than sent away," I said. "I don't know what is going on, but I know I don't want to leave my friends. You don't have to tell me what is going on, but I don't want to go away. But I do want to know what necklace I have that is so important."

"It's complicated," Grandmother explained. "But I think that we have no choice but to tell you about it now."

Sheena disappeared into the caravan and emerged a moment later with the lion necklace in her hand. She held it out to me and I took it. Grandmother told me the story of how she found me and why the necklace was so important.

"Joby," Grandmother warned me, "Do not wear that necklace anywhere where it can be seen in plain sight. Always remember to keep it hidden well. We will not send you away, but you must always have that necklace on you, and hidden well. We will make you a secret pocket."

"In my boot!" I almost screamed.

"What?" Sheena asked, confused.

"Look at my boot," I explained. "Do you see how the leather folds over at this part on the top? I can easily pull up the fold where we could sew in an extra patch of leather with a button so the pocket stays closed. Nobody would think to look there. If we had a secret pocket anywhere else, somebody might think to check for one."

"I told you she was smart," Grandmother beamed. "We will work on it right away, this minute."

Grandmother and Sheena got to work, fitting my boot with the little hidden pocket. When they had finished the last touches I slipped the lion necklace into it and closed it up. We all pulled and prodded on the pocket to make sure that the necklace was safe and that there were no adjustments needed. Then I put the boot on and folded the leather back down over my new secret stash to make sure that there wouldn't be a noticeable bulge underneath. It was perfect.

"Now you need to sleep for the rest of the night," Sheena said as she hurried me into my bed. "Take those boots off and put them beside your bed, within arm's reach." I did as Sheena told me and fell asleep within seconds. I wouldn't get to sleep for long.

I was awoken by the sound of horses whinnying and men yelling out orders. Sheena came rushing into the caravan.

"Put on your boots now, Joby," she rushed, "don't take them off until these men are gone. Do not say anything to anyone about the necklace."

She did not have to tell me any of this. I already knew. I knew that the necklace held some kind of significance to these men, or at least, one of them in particular.

"Out into the clearing, NOW!" One of the soldiers came bursting into our caravan. "Line up with the others."

Sheena and I did as we were told. I stood close to Sheena and held her hand, knowing that I would never again care that I was adopted by her. She was the one I needed to be near when I was this scared. I always knew that she would give her life to protect me. River lined up next to me, and grabbed my other hand.

"All girls, around age eight, come forward." This was the voice of the King of the North. He dismounted his horse to look us up and down as seven girls, including myself, came forward. I looked back at Sheena for reassurance. Her face looked slightly alarmed but she gave me a nod to let me know that everything was going to be all right.

The king walked up and down the line, eyeing each of us intently. As he came to each girl, he bent down and handed her a piece of candy.

"You have such pretty blond hair," he said soothingly to the first one, "go back to your mother."

He did this with four of the girls. He would bend down, hand her a piece of candy, and complement one of her features. Then he would tell her to go to her mother. Somehow I knew that he just wanted the three of us that were left to feel comfortable with him, so I put up my guard when he addressed the three of us that had not been sent back.

"I need to talk to you three," he said bending down and bringing us all closely into him, "I've left you for last, because you three are the most special. You have skin like a very lonely woman who is trying to find her daughter." I looked down at my brown skin and back at Sheena.

"Her daughter would be around eight-years-old now," he continued, "the same age as you three girls. I need to find her daughter and bring her back to her mother. She told me that her daughter would be with a tribe, because that is who she left her with. She gave the girl a necklace before she left her." He reached into his pocket and pulled a ring with a lion identical to the one I had hidden in my boot.

"Do any of you girls recognize this symbol?" We all shook our heads no and I tried extra hard to wipe any trace of recognition from my face.

The king looked annoyed and enraged for a moment. Then he composed himself and put on his gentle act again.

"Where is your mother?" He asked the first girl. She pointed her out to him and he asked the second girl who pointed to her mother. Then he asked me. I pointed to

Sheena. He looked hard at Sheena and then again at me. He gave the other two girls candy and sent them back to their mothers, but he held on to me.

He motioned for Sheena to come over to him. As he spoke to her, he began handing me little candies, one after the other. I took them and ate them, although I felt that this probably wasn't a good sign.

"Where is this child's father?" He asked her very forcefully. "I see father's with the other children, but there is no father for her."

"He died when I was four." I lied quickly when I saw Sheena struggling with her words. "Mommy still can't talk about it." Almost on cue, Sheena bowed her head in an excellent display of fake grief.

"I'm sorry," the king softened, "you both just look so much like someone that I know. It just seems like too much of a coincidence." He reached out his hand towards Sheena's face and traced the unique scar that she had on her chin before seemingly decided that we weren't what he was looking for. He began to walk to his horse, but stopped before mounting it.

"Still," he said, his mind obviously troubled, "it wouldn't hurt to be sure. Show my men to your caravan. I'm sorry but I think it should be searched just in case."

"And search the girl and her mother," he ordered his men as they began to follow us. "Make sure you check everything. That girl is probably the most likely candidate that we have come upon so far."

Sheena and I spent the next couple of hours pulling everything out of our caravan for the men to search. They came in and out of it many times, looked in every crevice, pulled up boards, shook out blankets and clothing, and checked in every pocket. Then they searched us. They checked our clothing inside and out, they made me pull off my boots, and they checked inside. They did the same for Sheena. They never pulled up the leather to reveal my little pocket. Then as quickly as they had come, they were gone. I watched them ride away into the forest, and couldn't help but notice the king looking back, glaring at me suspiciously until we could no longer see each other.

"We should finish the clearing," Grandmother addressed the tribe when they were out of earshot. "We should be safe from them now that they've already searched us and know that we don't have what they want." She looked at me and winked, and I smiled at her. It was a fake smile, because even at eight-years-old I knew that it was far from over. I could tell by the look in the king's eyes as he was riding away.

I slept that night in a constant fit of nightmares, all about being taken away and never returning to the forest. I do not remember much about them, except for a growing sense of desperation that never seemed to subside. I always tried to get back to the forest, but the chain from the necklace was holding me back, and the lion was standing guard in case I somehow escaped those chains. His green jewel of an eye was glittering and glowering at me in hatred.

"Wake up," Sheena was shaking me as the lion was getting ready to pounce, "we have training to do today."

"Training?" I asked groggily. "What sort of training?"

"Every kind of training that you could possibly think of." Sheena sighed. "I was going to wait, but after last night I am not going to chance leaving you defenseless."

"I was going to gather some stuff for the tribe with River today," I protested. "Grandmother said that all the children had to help gathering firewood and the little stuff so the adults can finish the clearing."

"Grandmother has made an exception," Sheena snapped. "And from now on, you will not be doing chores with the children. You will be learning how to do things with the adults. You know as much and more than many of the adults in this tribe, and so now you must learn how to act like an adult. I wouldn't have wished this for you, but you will have very little time to be young anymore. It's just the way things are."

I got up out of bed and got dressed. I carefully put on my boots and lifted up the leather flap to check that my secret pocket was still intact and that the necklace was safe inside. Then I went into the clearing where the tribe was preparing and eating breakfast.

The adults looked at me with pity in their eyes. They knew that today was the day I would be forced to grow up. The tribe always wanted the children to be able to stay young until they were at least age twelve, but my current circumstances would not allow me that luxury. I didn't care because I was excited about my new role in the tribe. I would soon learn that it wasn't as good as I thought it would be when the children's chores were done and they ran off into the forests to play, and I would still be stuck beside Sheena and the others, learning new skills and working until dark to finish everything that needed to be done. The only perk was that I was allowed to choose my own bedtime when the other children my age were forced to go to sleep.

River seemed to notice that I was unhappy and lonely. Even though I was constantly surrounded by other adults that were sharing the same chores that I was involved in, and Sheena was training me every second that I didn't have something that needed to be done, I didn't have anyone that I could actually talk to. The age difference between the adults and me was painfully obvious as they spoke of things that I had absolutely no interest in, so River asked the tribe if he could grow up as well. The request was met at first with opposition, but as the days went by and the adults saw how unhappy I was, they caved.

The way it is in a tribe is that fathers usually train their sons, and mothers usually train their daughters in hunting and fighting skills. River asked for special permission to be trained by Sheena. Even though this was an outrageous request by anyone's standards, the tribe gave in to this as well because they felt I needed as much support as possible, and River seemed to be exactly the push I needed in the right direction. So River and I spent most of our waking moments together, and it began to circulate around the tribe that we would probably end up married one day.

Sheena would train River and me against each other in hand-to-hand combat. River seemed to be better than me at that. He also picked up foraging skills faster. I was better at everything else. I could throw a knife at a target and string and shoot a bow better. My hunting skills were always two steps ahead of his, and my tracking was close to Sheena's abilities before we had been training for a month.

River wasn't bad at training; I was just always one step ahead of him. He seemed to get more and more irritated with me as I would try to explain something to him that I was better at. Soon I realized that I was bruising his ego, so instead of trying to help him out I began to tease him about it. That seemed to minimalize our fights. He always took being made fun of lightly, but he couldn't stomach someone who he thought was the same as him trying to teach him something that they learned at the same time.

So River and I grew into adults together. In the morning and early afternoons we did chores with the adults. In the late afternoons and early evenings we trained hard with Sheena. In the night we sat around the fire with the others, trying to stay awake and take advantage of the one thing that we had over the other kids our ages: our free will over bedtime. Most of the time we only made it ten minutes, but that was the good thing about doing it together. Those ten minutes each night were our happiest in the day. Perhaps that is why the adults loved them so much.

CHAPTER THREE

TROUBLE IN THE TOWNS

Four years had passed with little excitement in the tribe. River and I had nearly completed training when the rest of children our age were just beginning. We would sit and joke about them, and couldn't hide our jealousy. Although they were starting their training, it wouldn't be like ours. They would be gradually pushed into it little by little, and it would be more like a game for them. They wouldn't feel the full force of training until they were sixteen. It would be an occasional interruption for them. I was thrust into training full force out of necessity, and River out of loyalty.

I sometimes wondered if River held any animosity toward me, but if he did, he never once let on. He seemed to like being around me, even in the thick of the training. He told me once that he wouldn't want to go through training with anybody but me, and that is why he asked for it when he was eight.

So River and I worked together, watching the others struggling with their new workload, and giving them impossible chores that we knew they would have a problem finishing. We called it "weeding out the weaklings" and the others our age put up with it because they saw that we could do the work, and they didn't want to be outdone by us. The only reason we could do the work was because we had been doing it for four years. We didn't tell them this. Eventually, Grandmother caught on, and sent us on a hunting trip to keep us away from the others.

"I thought she would never catch on!" River laughed hysterically as we headed deep into the forest. "She just kept running around asking them, why are you trying to do this?"

"I'm surprised not one of them said anything to her until now," I laughed back.

"Man, they are going to hate us when she explains to them that those chores that we had been giving them are reserved for those that have built up their muscles for like two years!" River was holding himself up by a tree by this time.

"Well, let's go get some game and bring it back for the tribe." I smiled. "Time to grow up now. Let's get serious."

River straightened up and grabbed his gear, which had now fallen by his side. We always made time for a laugh, but I always had to be there to get us on a serious track again. That is why River and I worked well together. He was there to add a little fun to life, so that everything didn't seem so hopeless. Then I would turn around and get us back to what we needed to do. River was humanity and I was survival. I doubt either of us would have survived so long without the other. Even when I was alone I would think about River and be able to make it through whatever problem I was having at the moment.

We walked through the forests, shooting small animals with our arrows. There didn't seem to be any large game around today. It didn't matter; the trip wasn't one of necessity at this point. There was plenty of food back at the clearing. We were sent out for the sanity of the rest of the tribe. I doubt we would have shot a deer even if we had seen one. Sometimes they are just nice to watch.

"Let's pick some of these wild berries here," River said, stopping by a bush. "The tribe hasn't had berries for a while. This is the first bush I have come to since we moved to this clearing."

"Good idea," I agreed and we began to pick the berries and drop them into our pouches.

There was a rustling sound as we stood at the bush picking as much as we could fit without squishing them all together. We paid no attention to it at first because it was the same as the sound of a small animal rustling around. Then it wasn't. We heard the voice of a small child calling out to us. We turned around and saw a little boy of about age five. We could tell by the look of his clothing that he was the member of a tribe.

"Did you hear?" he gasped excitedly. "The King of the North has died."

"No," I said, "how did you get here? Do you need help finding your way back to your tribe?"

"You don't know?" He frowned. "All the tribes have been sticking close to this area. The king has forced us into this little patch. We've all been around here for two years while he's been following one tribe around. He didn't want the tribe to get lost within our tribes, so he made sure to keep us in one place while he just let them wander. Doesn't seem fair to me."

"I think we might have been the wandering tribe," I sighed heavily. "I'm sorry."

"It doesn't matter anymore," the boy exclaimed. "Now we can all leave!" Then the boy ran off, undoubtedly to tell the other captive tribes the good news.

"How did we not know about this?" River pondered incredulously.

"No communication between us and the other tribes," I answered. "The king wanted it that way. He was planning something, and I want to know what it was. I knew it was too good to be true that he never bothered us again after that day."

"We better get back and tell Grandmother," River sighed. "And I thought we were going to have a day off today."

We went back to the camp and dropped off our kills and the berries with the tribe members who were preparing the meal for that day. They seemed grateful for the fresh fruit and promised to make a good meal of it for the night. As we made our way to Grandmother, we were stopped many times by others wanting to know the exact location of the berries so when it was their turn to collect the food they would know where to get it from.

"Grandmother," I leaned over and whispered anxiously in her ear when we finally made it to her. "River and I have something important to discuss with you. It is very important that we speak privately." This was the way that we did things in the tribe. If someone would come upon some disturbing information, it was always run by Grandmother first, and she would decide what to do with it. This would prevent widespread panic among the people in our tribe, and also stupid mistakes that had gotten other tribes wiped out entirely.

"Grandmother, I need to find out what was going on," I told her after we had explained what the boy in the forest had told us. "I

need to go to town. It won't be as dangerous
any more now that the king is gone. Let me go
and I will come back with any information that
I can."

"I will let you go with me," Grandmother
agreed. "River will also come since he knows
what is going on as well. We will tell the
tribe that the king has died and it is now
safe to go into town and start trading again.
It will only be us three and we will bring all
the extra materials we have collected over the
last four years as a pretense for us going. I
will tell the tribe that you two are coming
along to give the new trainees a chance to
relax. It was lucky that you two have been so
much trouble lately, otherwise that might not
go over very well. Many people would like to
go into town. While we are haggling, we will
all listen for some clues that might explain
why we have been spied on for the last four
years."

"I know, Grandmother," I said, eyes
downcast. Grandmother shot me a warning look
and then looked over at River, who was
obliviously picking apart a blade of grass.
Then I remembered that River did not know that
the king was actually after me. I stayed
quiet after that.

Grandmother explained everything to the
tribe as we had discussed. There were a few
complaints among the adults, who wanted to
accompany us to town, but Grandmother quickly
blew off their arguments and they got the
message that she had already made up her mind.
Even though there was always one person who
disagreed with Grandmother, they all had
enough respect for her to realize that when
she made up her mind, that was the law of the
tribe. She had always kept us safe, and

whatever she was doing right now, was for the good of the tribe as a whole.

We set off for the town, which was about a day's journey out of the forest, with all the goods that were piled up high on wagons led by horses. There were four years of goods that we didn't dare bring into the towns to trade for fear of running into the king and his men. Now that we didn't have to worry about the king, we didn't see the harm in bringing everything in. We were sure that the towns would take at least some of it off of our hands.

We settled down and made a fire when it began to get dark. We would have to finish the journey in the morning. We only had about two miles to go, which took a little longer in the woods, but we knew that we didn't want to get to town in the night. Members of a tribe are always a little weary of spending the night somewhere besides the forest.

"Grandmother!" A voice called excitedly out of the darkness. Grandmother stood up. A young man of about twenty ran out of the forest and into her arms as they opened up.

"This is my daughter's son!" Grandmother explained to River and me. "She married a man from town and Joseph here returned to the forest, although he lives in a house, not a caravan."

"What are you doing so close to town, Grandmother?" Joseph asked, eyeing our load. "It's not safe to trade."

"But the king is dead now, Joseph," Grandmother replied.

"It's not the king you have to worry about now, Grandmother," Joseph explained, "It's the people. For the last four years that king has been on a frantic search for a slave girl's child. Nobody knows why. But since he's been looking his men and him have been using up a lot of resources in the towns. Now the towns have nothing themselves. If you go into town with all of this, you might lose your life for it. At least when the king was alive, there was a little order in the towns."

"Is it as bad as all that?" Grandmother sighed, looking more tired than I have ever seen her look before. Joseph nodded.

"Then shouldn't we bring it in anyway? No trade required?" I asked. "We've always been taught to take care of each other. Shouldn't we treat the people in the towns the same as we would treat each other?"

"Joby is right, Joseph," Grandmother replied, looking at her grandson.

"Then let's do it this way," Joseph compromised. "We will bring everything to my house, and you will bring one small load at a time. Each load that you bring you will promise that you will be back with more. That should keep you safe. We will bring the first load tonight when there are very few people awake. That way the word will spread by morning that more is coming."

We each grabbed an armful of goods and carried it into the town. We were swamped as soon as we arrived. People were reaching out for blankets, clothing, and anything they could get their hands on. We were almost trampled by the few people who were awake in the night. Joseph had been right about coming at the hour that we did. I don't know how we would have survived the stampede if everybody had been awake.

"Listen," Joseph called out to the group when our hands had been emptied. "We will return tomorrow with more supplies. Please compose yourselves by then, and make a point to tell others to do so as well. We cannot bring supplies if we are not in the shape to do so." The group all murmured their agreement and went off in separate directions to spread the word.

We came back the next day as we had promised with armfuls of more supplies. We came back six times that day. By the time we were done, we were all sweating and it was clear that Grandmother needed to rest. We still had more at Joseph's house, and we decided that since by this point the crowds of people had managed to coax themselves into a more orderly way of ridding us of our goods, they could be trusted enough for us to bring the rest of the supplies in a wagon.

As we sat down to rest, watching the happy people show each other what they had gotten from us, I realized something else about them. They were all starving. Everything we had brought them would keep them warm in the night, would keep them clothed, and would help them do chores around the town, but nothing would feed them. My attention was focused very intently on a specific little girl, holding a tiny crying baby in her arms, while her mother was trying to get the infant to drink just a little water. The baby was dying of hunger. I thought about how no little girl should have to watch something like that.

"Grandmother," I began as I sat down beside her, not taking my eyes off the sad scene I was witnessing, "after we bring this last load, you go home and I'm going to stay here and see about hunting down some food for these people." Grandmother didn't even try to object.

"River will stay with you," she agreed, "and you will both stay with Joseph. If we leave the clearing, I will try to leave you a trail. One that only someone from the tribe would be able to recognize. We don't know that we are out of danger yet."

"Fine," I agreed, "are you ready to go yet?"

"I think I will just wait here," Grandmother panted. "I'm getting too old to do things like this anymore. You and River and Joseph will just have to bring the rest of the supplies back."

The three of us trudged into the forest after leaving Grandmother with some people who promised to do their best to liven her up a bit. On the way to the house I spotted a deer and shot it with my bow and arrow.

"It's not much," I told Joseph and River, "but it's a start. At least it's meat." Joseph walked over to the deer and threw it over his shoulders. I was happy to let him do it after the day that I had.

We loaded the fresh kill up onto the wagon and then decided to cover it a little with the other goods. We didn't know what kind of pandemonium would break out if the people of the town saw that deer sitting up there on the wagon, ready to be ripped apart and eaten. We thought it best to explain about the deer before the townspeople saw it, and to let them know that there would be more, and that River and I would train anyone who wanted to learn how to hunt and provide for the town before we left it again without giving them a way to keep themselves from going hungry. We never got a chance to tell them that there was even a deer to be eaten.

We heard the commotion from the trees before we knew what was going on. Joseph motioned for us to stop the wagon, but we didn't need to be told. We all crept close to the edge of the forest, peering through the trees, careful to keep ourselves hidden from sight until we knew what was going on.

The king's men were there, ravaging the town, stealing all the new goods that we had just passed among the people. In the middle of it all, was a boy who was a year or so older than I was, screaming out orders to the soldiers.

"Who is that?" I asked Joseph.

"That is the king's son," Joseph whispered back. "He's the new king. Everybody thought that he would be easy to get around. I guess we were all wrong on that."

"They complain about being poor," the boy king screamed, "and then we come and find them with all these riches. Let's show them what it is like to really be poor. Take everything! Kill anyone who objects."

I closed my eyes and prayed that nobody would object, but the years of neglect and oppression had finally gotten to the townspeople. There were so many of them putting up a fight that the boy king finally just gave the order to kill everybody.

"No!" I heard Grandmother shout. "Stop this! Please! We were just trying to help them!"

"Get out of there, Grandmother," I whispered under my breath. Grandmother just kept approaching the boy king. She made it to his horse, and grabbed the reins, and began to plead with him for the lives of all the townspeople. He seemed to listen to her for a moment, but then his mouth curled into an evil little sneer and he pulled out a sword and ran her through. She held onto the reins a little longer, despite the pain and confusion in her face, and then he kicked her and she fell over onto her back, still looking up at him in horror. He rode away, looking for his next victim.

"Grandmother!" I screamed and broke away from Joseph and River, who were trying to hold me back. I don't ever remember running that fast toward or away from something before or even since that day that I ran to Grandmother's side to be with her in her final moments of life. I was there to catch her final words that she would ever speak to anybody. I took her hand in mine and leaned in close to hear her above the chaos that was happening around me. The last words of a member of a tribe are the most important to hear. They are the words that they will be remembered by forever. I didn't expect what I was about to hear from Grandmother.

"Tell the tribe that they have to take this king down," Grandmother whispered. "We live in the forests for a reason, and that is to come out when we are needed the most. Right now we are needed the most."

"I will, Grandmother," I promised. Then her body went limp and I let go of her hand. I felt a surge within me and pulled the sword out of Grandmother's body as one of the soldiers ran toward me, with his own sword exposed.

I'd never been particularly good at hand-to-hand combat, and I had never handled a sword before. The tribe prefers to carry lighter weapons, ones that can easily be moved, but I had never been an ordinary member of the tribe. I found my niche with the sword almost as soon as I picked it up, which was a good thing because I was able to protect myself as the soldier bared down on me. I managed to kill my very first enemy that day, and that kill would give me the confidence to be one of the most dangerous people that the new king would have to try to eliminate, at least for a while.

After killing the soldier, I looked around at what was happening, and I realized how outnumbered I was. I decided that I could fight another day and began to run back toward the forest.

"Stop her! She has my sword," the boy king screamed, and I looked up to see him rushing toward me on his horse. I had to think fast, he was gaining on me. I wouldn't be able to escape him on foot. I saw a long, sturdy piece of broken wood in front of me. I grabbed it and waited for him to get close. When he was within feet of me, I quickly positioned the ragged edges of it toward the horse's neck. It was hard to hold onto it tightly, but my muscles had been well toned from the years of hard labor and the broken wood jabbed firmly into the horse's neck. The horse threw the boy king as it did a somersault over its head.

"That was my favorite horse!" The boy king fumed as he glowered at me and got to his feet. "You will pay for that!"

"You have to catch me first," I sneered and took off running again toward the forest. He could have followed me, but as I ran off I heard him screaming for the men to bring him another horse.

I was only about six feet from the forest when I heard a woman cry out for help. I

turned and saw the woman holding the hungry
baby I had seen earlier.

"I cannot find my little girl," the woman
begged, "and I can't leave her. Please take
my baby with you until I can find my little
girl."

"You can't be thinking about going back
into that!" I yelled at her incredulously.
"You will be killed!"

"I know," the woman replied desperately,
"but I can't live knowing that I left my
daughter in that. Please take my baby." She
handed the pathetic looking thing over to me,
and I stared at her only for a moment before
looking up to see that the boy king had
finally gotten a horse and was heading toward
me and the woman. Without thinking, I tucked
the baby as securely as I could into my shirt
and ran off into the forest. I turned around
as I heard a crack and realized that the
mother of the baby I was holding had been
bludgeoned to death by the boy king. I
realized that now I was responsible for this
child's life and didn't look back again until
I was sure I was safely hidden in the forest.

There was a hollow cave that I knew of
nearby. I had seen it and mentioned it to the
others on our journey to the town. It was
well hidden, and only visible if you were to
stumble upon it, which is exactly what I had
accidently done. I had told the others that
it would be a nice place to hide if we ever
got into any trouble, and so when the sound of
men following me had subsided, I decided to
back track and go there to spend the night. I
was relieved when I found River and Joseph
already there, and I could tell that they were
happy to see me.

Then I realized something that horrified me; the baby that I was carrying had never made a sound the entire time I was running through the woods. I thought to myself that the baby must surely be dead if it was not disturbed by the abrupt movements and absence of her mother. I quickly brought her out of my shirt and looked at her. Her eyes were open, looking drowsily at me. She didn't seem to be bothered by anything.

"We need to get some food into that thing," Joseph said urgently, "she's going to die if we don't. She's so listless."

"What do we have?" I asked, panicked. "What can she eat?"

"Berries," Joseph replied. "I think she might be able to eat berries. She's not too young, I don't think. If we squish them up good I think that would be fine." So we mashed up the berries as well as we could. We fed them to her slow, knowing that she had been hungry for some time and we didn't want to make her sicker, and we didn't know if berries were something that you could give to a starving person. We had never seen anyone hungry before today. She seemed to like them, and she ate them well.

We stayed in the cave for a couple of days feeding the baby whatever we thought she might be able to handle. Her small size made her look younger than she was as we realized when she smiled for the first time and we saw a mouth full of teeth. We realized that she was probably close to two years old, although her small body made her look like she wasn't even a year old yet.

"We need to go home now," River told me the morning we left the cave. "We can leave the baby with Joseph."

"No," I argued, "I'm keeping her. She knows me, and I saved her. Besides, I don't think Joseph can go back to his house anyway. It's too close to the town. He will have to come back with us as well."

"I think you are right," Joseph agreed.

"Okay then," River sighed. I got the feeling he didn't like Joseph too well. "We'll just go back and get the goods and then head home."

"NO!" Joseph and I both yelled at the same time. We looked at each other in amusement for a moment.

"We can't go back for the supplies," I laughed, anxiously, "the soldiers probably already found it and picked it clean. What's more is they are probably waiting for the owners to come back and claim it so they can do whatever they did back in the town to them."

"It's bound to be a dangerous time right now," Joseph continued. "The boy king needs to assert his dominance over the land so there is going to be a few casualties. He isn't going to take anything lightly."

"Fine," River fumed. "Let's just go."

We picked up the last of our belongings and put them in our packs. Joseph offered to carry mine so that I didn't have to deal with the weight of the baby on top of the weight of my pack. She really didn't weigh that much, but I could tell he really wanted to do something to help me, so I didn't refuse.

When we returned to the clearing, we found it being packed up by the tribe. I had a feeling that the king and his men had found their way through here and had scared them enough to want to move on. Sheena confirmed my suspicions when she ran up to me and gave me a hug that spoke relief.

"Grandmother is dead," I informed her. Her embrace was abruptly broken as she pushed me away to look into my eyes, hoping to see a glimmer of untruth in them.

"Are you sure?" Sheena asked, already knowing the answer. When the king and his men came through they had mentioned to the tribe about what they may have done in the town. They had all thought that we all had been lost, which is why they weren't going to wait around for our return to pack up and leave.

"I need to talk to all of the adults, and those children who have started their training," I urged, "it's important. It's about Grandmother's last words."

That night when all of the young children had been sent to bed, the rest of the tribe sat up and I explained to them what Grandmother had ordered me to. We all decided that we would have to unite all the tribes and come together as a whole. Training would be more fierce, and hunting and gathering would have to be largely taken over by those who could not fight yet, but still had some training, no matter how weak it was.

After the meeting, Sheena and I walked back to our caravan. I stared down at the sleeping baby that I had put to bed in the old wooden box that had been my crib twelve years before. Sheena asked me at that point where I had gotten her. She knew that asking me before than would have been too much for me to explain with everything else that had been going on. I broke down and cried and told her the entire story, and when I was done she hugged me and stroked my hair like she hadn't done since it was decided that I would become an adult.

"What are you going to name her?" She asked me gently.

"Cub," I answered immediately.

"Why Cub?"

"Because when I became an adult by necessity I found out I had a lion," I replied, "and now that I've become an adult by choice, I find that I have a cub." Sheena needed no more explanation than that.

CHAPTER FOUR

STARTING A WAR

Sheena became the new leader of the tribe. She had always contributed the most to the group, and she always seemed to have knowledge that nobody else did. It was an easy decision for everybody to come to that she would be the one that everyone would follow. Twelve years ago, they might have come to a different conclusion, but when I was given to her, she changed into a person that everybody could approach. She had all of the characteristics that made Grandmother a leader.

The first thing that Sheena did was to give everybody a job. We had a war coming, and we all needed to be prepared for it. We had people hunting and gathering all day long. Then there were people who preserved and packed the food. It was a big job, but it needed to be done because we wouldn't always have the time to do these things when the fighting started.

We also decided that since we would have to be ready to move at a moment's notice, we could no longer live in caravans. People began to use the leather that we would normally take to trade and sew them into tents that could be taken down and put up within mere minutes. Everybody was to have one. We would move from place to place and leave no indication that we had been there.

After all of the preparations had been assigned to people, Sheena came to River,

Joseph, and me. It seems that we were to have a very special assignment.

"I need you three to go from tribe to tribe and spread the word," Sheena explained. "It's going to be dangerous, but I know that if you could get out of that town and bring a baby with you without being caught, I know that you will be able to do this." We agreed to do it, although I wrestled with the thought of leaving Cub behind for the first time since I had brought her back to the tribe with me. Sheena promised that she would be well taken care of, and I had no doubts that she would. What bothered me was I felt like I was abandoning her, and I didn't want her to feel that way.

I spent a little extra time with Cub that night before I left. I explained to her that I would be back when I could, but that I might be gone for a long time. I know she didn't understand anything I was saying, and after a while she just fell asleep. I held her until Joseph and River came to tell me that it was time for us to leave.

I laid Cub down in her little box and took one of my shirts and wrapped it around her. I hoped that in the next few days that would help her to not miss me as much. I kissed her little forehead and promised her once again that I would be back. I wonder if I was trying to reassure myself of that as much as I was her.

"Be careful," Sheena whispered as she touched her forehead to mine, "find a way to stay hidden at all times."

"I will," I promised, "and take care of my new sister." Sheena nodded her head in agreement.

River, Joseph, and I decided that we would travel by climbing the trees and moving between them. The forest was so dense that unless you were traveling by the trail you could just step from tree to tree. We knew that it wouldn't be smart to take the trail anyway, because that would be the path that the boy king and his men would take.

Every once in a while, we would hear a rustling, so we would always stop and stay very still. We would watch and listen to see what the noise was. It was usually an animal making its way through the forest. Every once in a while it was a scout who was looking for someone. It was rarely more than one person, but we were still careful to not let them see us, just in case there were more soldiers, out of our sight.

Little by little, we made it to each tribe. We spoke with the leader of each. Some of them were reluctant to agree to go to war, but when we spoke about what had happened in the town, they all eventually agreed. We found fifty tribes in all, although we knew there must be more out there somewhere. We told the leaders to spread the word if they ever come across any tribe that had not heard about our war yet.

And then, just like that, it began. We would meet others from the tribes, here and there. But every tribe had its own strategy and we were all slippery and knew how to disappear easily into the forest. We all had our ways of getting information, and passing it along to one another with nobody else knowing. We stopped living in the clearings, and instead we used the rest of the overgrown forest to keep us from being easily caught. I brought Sheena and Cub back to the cave we had hidden in when we escaped from the town, and we made that our home.

Cub learned early on that she couldn't be out in the open, and that she really couldn't be anywhere without Sheena or I close by. She never was in any real danger, but she was always weary of strangers because of the constant nagging from both Sheena and I to stay away from them. She was nothing like I was at a young age. Sheena said I was fierce and independent from the day that I learned how to walk. Cub was cautious and very loving. She was the reason I could not bear to think about not coming home. As long as I was home with her, there was nothing else wrong in the world.

I couldn't always be home with Cub, however, but when I wasn't Sheena usually was. There were only a handful of times when Joseph would come over to the cave and take care of Cub when neither Sheena nor I could be there. We began to joke that Joseph was her father, and he could have been. While Sheena and I could have easily been mother and daughter, Joseph and Cub could have easily been father and daughter. They were both blond with the most amazing blue eyes that I had ever seen. I realized that I had started to care for Joseph very deeply for the way that he looked so much like Cub.

The year had drug on and on, and I watched Cub grow from the safety of our cave. She slowly gained the strength she should have already had, and eventually she learned how to walk, and then she was running before I knew it. I began to teach her the things that I thought an older sister would teach a younger sibling. We played games, and I made her little dolls and presents. I mainly made her toys that would easily keep her quiet, even though I really didn't need to; she was just a quiet kid. Then one day she said my name out of the blue. It was one of the happiest moments of my life. For a long time, we didn't know if she would ever be able to speak. She learned things at a slower rate than all of the other kids, but from that point on, she seemed to keep up with them pretty well. It was a turning point in her life.

"There is going to be a real battle!" River came running into the cave one night. I shot him a warning look. Cub had just fallen asleep.

"I'm sorry," he apologized, "but we all need to be there. Joseph is coming to watch Cub since he hasn't had much experience with anything else." River made a point to emphasize this last statement.

"Okay," I whispered, "I will go wake Sheena. Where is it going to be?"

"In the town where it all started!" River announced triumphantly. "Some of the king's men are camped out there waiting for instructions from the king. I guess they got separated while searching the woods and they decided to just go back there. Some of the spies from another tribe saw them discussing it, and they sent a messenger out to find the king's group. We intercepted the messenger, and let's just say that the king will never get that message!"

River decided that he was going to go on ahead to the battle before Joseph showed up to take care of Cub. Sheena and I both decided to wait for him. We took turns watching over Cub, both knowing that this was possibly the last time either of us would make it back to see her ever again.

"If Sheena and I don't make it back," I told Joseph, "you can pass for her father. Your best bet for making a good life for her would be to jump from town to town and act like you belong until you reach the next kingdom over. The east and south are no good, try for the west, but if it comes down to surviving, do what you have to."

"I will," Joseph promised me, "but try to come back, Joby, Cub needs you."

"I will do what I have to do," I told him. I made him no promises. I wasn't sure if I would be able to keep them. For a year I had been preparing myself for the possibility that this war might be the end of me. It would possibly be the end of everyone I knew. It could even be possibly the end of the tribes in the forest and the way of life that we all held so dear.

Sheena and I set off into the dark night. We made our way to the ghost town filled with soldiers and our friends and neighboring tribes fighting each other to the death. As we got closer we noticed that there were no sounds of battle, only the sound of eerie, restless quiet. We came to the edge of the trees and peered out into the still town. There was nobody there. There were no tribes, and no soldiers. It was as if time had stopped and removed every person from within the town.

"What is going on here?" Sheena marveled, confused. She began to step out of the trees and into the town.

"No," I urged her. "Stop. Something is wrong." Sheena shrunk back into the trees. She had learned by now to trust my instincts.

I had been using them for a year, and they had paid off for me every time.

Across the town, in another thick of trees we saw and heard rustling. We watched as members of one of our neighboring tribes tiptoed out of the safety of the forest. They spoke to each other in hushed voices and then their voices began to get a little louder as the complained to each other about misinformation and how much time they had wasted to get here. Sheena cupped her hand over her mouth as she saw soldiers silently creep out of the houses behind them and sneak up on them. We could not warn them for fear they would come to find us, and then we would not be able to send the word out that it was a trap. Instead, we watched in horror as every single one of them was knocked out cold and then tied up and drug into the houses.

"What are they going to do with them?" I whispered.

"I don't know," Sheena answered back. "Let's go and warn everybody before they come here."

We spent the rest of the night starting the message and spreading it across the forest that the battle at the town was a trap. I hoped that I would find River in my quest, but he never turned up and I realized that he was probably already taken hostage, or possibly killed when he went on ahead of us.

"Don't worry," Joseph tried to reassure me when we made it back home to the cave, "they are probably just taking them as slaves. Rumor is that the king is pulling workers from the fields to make more soldiers. They are sweating there in the north. They are running short of food, and people to produce it, but if the king allows people to go back to the fields, then he will be left wide open to attack and he will lose this war. Joby, we are winning this."

I felt a bit better about the war we were fighting, but it would take me years to get over the loss of River. I never thought I would ever see him again.

CHAPTER FIVE

THE WAR TAKES A NASTY TURN

We had been fighting for nearly four years. I felt bad for Cub because she rarely saw the outside of our cave. She never complained and I was happy for it, because I don't think I could have taken another minute of not living out in the open if it wasn't for her.

I thought to myself on many occasions that life shouldn't be like this for me. Here I was, sixteen years old, and everything I had been for the past 8 years shouldn't have happened until this year. I didn't have time to feel jealousy for the little ones this time though, and even if I did, the jealousy would be unfounded. We were all suffering. Everybody was growing up. Nobody had time to be a kid.

I thought about what it was like before all of the trouble had started. River and I used to climb the trees and yell at the top of our lungs as if we were some crazy animals living up there. Now there were no sounds of children in the trees. There were no sounds at all. Everybody was completely quiet. Noise was something we couldn't afford because the king and his men could be anywhere. I felt sorrow, rather than jealousy for the kids of the tribe.

Sometime in the middle of all the fighting, Joseph came to live with us. It became easier to have him always there, because we needed to be able to leave at a moment's notice. It wasn't that Joseph could not have joined in the fighting; he was just better at things at home. He was tenderer with Cub than either Sheena or I was. We all loved Cub, but Sheena and I never possessed the right kind of softness that Joseph had, the kind that the sensitive little girl needed. Maybe it was the fact that they were both born within town. Townspeople seemed to be more emotional than the people in the forests.

Joseph and I enjoyed each other's company very much. He never fully took the place of River as my best friend, neither was our relationship ever the same as it had been with River. Joseph and I reacted with each other in a much more soothing manner. We spent our moments together softly, whereas River and I were in constant competition with each other. We must have fallen in love sometime in the last year, but I don't remember it happening. One morning I had woken up and decided that I had loved him, and I told him so. He returned the emotion, and we had become partners. It was simple like that in the tribe.

After our mutual declaration of adoration for each other, going off to fight became harder on everybody. Joseph visibly showed his emotions as I would leave the cave, and that had an effect on Cub, who was now six and able to effectively show her emotions. This stressed Sheena and me out as we left, because she would beg us not to go. By showing his emotions, something he had been able to keep silent until we had come together, Cub had realized that Joseph was afraid for us to leave. She realized at this point that we were in danger.

Cub began to fake illnesses and injuries when it was time for us to leave. We caught on after the first few incidents, but she never stopped trying just the same. We tried to tell her every time we left how far ahead we were in the war. Nobody could find where the tribes had hidden themselves and there was always very little danger on our side. The king and his men were slowly being wiped out by hunger, disease, and us. It wouldn't be long and we would have won.

Then one day, it all changed. They had somehow been led to where we would hold meetings. The word spread fast among the tribes that there was a trap waiting there, but it was too late. Half of all our people had been captured and brought back to the town, which was where they had their base. The rest of us decided that we would attempt a rescue mission to save the others. We were all going to attack at full force on their camp that night and hope that we would take them by surprise to such an extent that they wouldn't be able to defend themselves. We thought about wiping them all out right there at that moment.

They had expected us, though. That was the reason they were taking our people alive, instead of killing them. They wanted to give us hope so that they could snuff us out, all at once. My story should have ended here, if it weren't for the intense need of the king to seek revenge.

We were all waiting in the trees, watching for a sign that it would be a good time to attack. We saw a few men standing guard around the camp, and we assumed the others would be sleeping soundly in the houses. We didn't see or hear the soldiers creeping up behind us, swords drawn and ready to attack. Apparently, they had been watching us to learn something from us.

I felt the sword being poked into my back. I took a deep breath and turned around slowly. I watched as the rest of my friends did the same. I looked over at Sheena, waiting for a signal as to what to do. She stood there like a stone, silent and pale. We had spent so many years reveling at how unorganized and dumb they seemed to be and we never expected to be taken like this.

We were pushed into the center of the town by the swords. I heard some of my people crying and begging for their lives. They weren't harming anybody, though. Then they brought the rest out from the houses and pushed them to the center with the rest of us. I prayed for a quick death. I would not get one.

Then he came out. He swaggered over to us all, with a smug look on his face. He laughed obnoxiously, rubbing it in our face that he had won. He had grown tall, and he wasn't a boy anymore. I looked him over. He had tan skin with black hair and green eyes. He wouldn't have been bad looking, if it weren't for the evil smile. You could tell just by looking at him that he was a tyrant. He could either get what he wanted by how nice he could look, or by scaring you with that evil smile of his.

He walked around us in a circle. He was looking for someone, I could tell by his eyes. I instinctively moved deeper into the crowd because I knew it was me, and I was afraid of what would happen to the rest if he found me. I knew that we were all dead, but I wanted it to be quick and painless for us.

"Your Majesty," I heard a soldier call from far away, towards the forest. His voice sounded amused. "Look what we found hiding in a little hole in the ground." I peered over the crowd to see what was going on, and was horrified to see Joseph holding on to a frightened Cub, while being pushed into the group.

"No!" I screamed and attempted to make a run for them, but two hands caught me and dropped me to the ground. Those hands belonged to the king. He frowned at me for a moment, and then his face twisted in recognition and he sneered at me with that evil smile of his. I felt like he was taking my breath away, and began to panic.

"Let's play a little game," he said to his soldiers, all the while never taking his eyes off of me. This game was for my benefit. "This girl right here is going to choose which of these people lives or dies. She gets to choose five people out of this crowd, who will get to go on their way if they pledge allegiance to me." He held out his hand to let me up.

I didn't know what to do. I was afraid to choose Sheena, Cub, and Joseph because the king knew who I was and would probably take revenge on me by hurting the people I loved. I decided that I couldn't chance not choosing them because they were the people that I loved the most, and I had to try to save them at least. I picked them out of the crowd and they were instructed to stay separate from everybody else.

Then I had to pick two more. I didn't have any particular system about doing it. I just closed my eyes and pointed in two directions. Those two were pulled forcefully from the group and placed with my family.

"Now," the king ordered, "kill the rest." I was pushed into the group and the king ordered a halt.

"NO!" He bellowed. "NOT HER! I didn't make myself clear, she is going to live and see all the lives that she could not have saved. You can take the other five away. They don't have to watch this." They took my family and the two others away somewhere. Only Sheena fought them. Joseph was trying to stay strong for Cub, and the other two were just too happy to be alive to do any more fighting that day.

One by one I was forced to watch as members from the tribe were executed while he held my face in their direction so that I could not look away. At some point, I collapsed to the ground and tried to tuck my head so that he could not force it back to the awful sight. He made the soldiers stop until he could. I saw every drop of blood spill from each of their bodies. It only made me angry, and I vowed to myself to get back at him somehow. Then finally, it was all over.

He forced me into the house where they were keeping my family and the other two that I had "chosen" to live. When I looked at them, I could not hold in my emotions anymore. I fell to the floor and began to cry tears of anger, and sadness all at the same time. Joseph rushed to me and put his arms around me to comfort me.

"Leave her," the king told him forcefully. Joseph wouldn't budge. "I said leave her!" The king tried to pull Joseph up by his hair, but Joseph was too large, and he stubbornly stayed planted by my side. I watched in horror as the king pulled his head back and produced a knife from his pocket. He sliced Joseph's neck in one quick motion, and Joseph fell to the floor, gasping for breath, and then he was dead.

I couldn't say anything, and so I did the only thing that I could. I lay there on Joseph's body, listening to the king screaming at me to get up. I didn't care if he killed me, too. I needed to spend a few last moments with Joseph, while his body was still warm. It took three men to pry me off of Joseph and pin me down to a chair, where I was tied up. They took his body away and I never saw him again.

I noticed at this point that Cub was crying hysterically. I looked at her and tried to give her a reassuring look, but I don't think that I managed it that well. I had hoped that she would never see anything this brutal. I felt like I had failed her.

"Show the three adults out and make sure they don't come back," the king told his men a moment later. "The little girl will stay with us." I began to get nervous again. I knew that whatever he was planning was going to be awful, but I hoped he wasn't heartless enough to kill Cub.

"Don't worry," he said to Sheena as she began to fight again, "I won't hurt the little girl. I need her."

"Just leave," I mouthed to Sheena as she looked at me, alarmed. She glanced suspiciously at the king one last time, and then she went with the others. I was glad that I knew she would be safe at least. She would probably form another attack in the future sometime. She might even save us all.

"Put the girl to bed," the king ordered his men. "I have to have a little chat with this one. Leave me alone with her."

"That girl is the one that you saved from the town a few years back, isn't it?" He asked as if he was looking for confirmation that he actually had the right person. I thought that I could go one of two ways: I could either deny that I knew what he was talking about, or I could tell the truth. I decided not to risk insulting his intelligence and nodded that he was on the right track. I was rewarded with a slap in the face.

"Where is my sword?" His eyes flashed angrily.

"What?" I winced as he threatened to hit me again.

"My sword," he screamed. "The one that you ripped out of the old woman and ran off with into the forest. What have you done with it?"

"You did all this to me because of a stupid sword?" I shouted. "You have got to be the most heartless bastard that ever lived."

"WHERE IS IT?"

"I don't know," I screeched. "I lost it while I was trying to escape from you!"

He began to pace back and forth in front of me. Every once in a while he would reach up and pull at his hair. This went on for about ten minutes and then he just stopped. He stared at the wall for a moment and then punched a hole in it. I jumped and he seemed to take notice of me again.

"That was my father's sword!" he informed me. "It was the only one that he ever used, and you lost it!" He kicked the chair that I was tied in over and I had no way to catch myself as my head hit the floor. I blacked out then and didn't wake up until the morning.

Cub was sitting over me when I woke up. She had been washed and dressed and very well taken care of. She cried and hugged me tight when she saw my eyes open, and I was glad to see that she had been unharmed.

"Cub," I whispered her name with appreciation. She held her finger to her lips to signal that she didn't want the others to know that I had woken up. It was too late.

I heard his footsteps walk over to where I was. He knelt down beside me so that I could see his face. He was more calm and composed than he had been the night before. I had a feeling that I wasn't going to like what he was about to tell me.

"You and Cub will be accompanying me back to my castle," he explained. "You are going to be an example of what happens when you try to stand up against me. Cub will be fine as long as you do everything that I tell you to do. In fact, she will be more than fine. She will have the best of everything and live a privileged life without any worries, unless you upset me. Then she will feel your punishment worse because she will have lived so good for so long. Do I have your agreement that you will not try anything on the journey or after?"

I nodded my agreement to him. There was nothing else I could do. It was at this moment that I feared the worst had truly happened. I knew without a shadow of a doubt that he had defeated me.

CHAPTER SIX

A NEW LIFE FOR CUB AND ME

He put me in a locked room our first day
there, and then he took Cub away to some other
part of the castle. The room was comfortable
enough, even though it was a prison. The bed
was soft and the bedding was warm. There was
a fireplace and plenty of wood, even though
the evening was warm enough and I wouldn't
need any fire that night. I wondered to
myself what kind of torture he thought he was
putting me through. I was being treated more
like a guest than a prisoner.

I was brought breakfast, lunch, and
supper. There was plenty of food. In fact,
there was more than enough food. It was clear
that he didn't plan on torturing me through
starvation. I began to get nervous about what
his plans were for me. Maybe he was just
lulling me into a false sense of security.
Maybe he was just planning on making me go
crazy wondering what he planned on doing to
me.

Evening came and so I lay down on the
bed. It was uncomfortable because I wasn't
used to something so soft. I decided to move
the bedding to the floor and sleep there.
That did the trick. It was more like my home.
I began to feel homesick almost immediately.
We always slept so close, the others and me.
Now here I was, alone. Even when I was out on
a mission, I was never alone. At the very
least, I had the sound of the forest to keep
me company. But it was strange here. There
were sounds, but no rustling of the leaves in

the trees. No wolves howling in the night.
No birds chirping. No whistling wind.
Instead, there were the sounds of footsteps in
the halls. Voices talking in hushed whispers.
There was a strange creaking here and there.
It was nothing like the forest.

I couldn't stop thinking about Sheena.
Even though I was alone, she must feel more
alone than me. At least I knew that Cub and I
were safe. Sheena would have no idea. She
would be out there, somewhere, hoping that we
were still alive.

Thinking about Sheena made me think about
the lullaby she used to sing to me when I was
small. We both sang it to Cub now. I thought
to myself that maybe if I sang the lullaby,
Cub would be close enough to hear it and
wouldn't be scared. I made up my mind that
this was the thing to do.

> *The rain pours down.*
> *The darkness is crying.*
> *But here we are warm, safe, and*
> *sound.*
> *As long as we have been living,*
> *day's dying.*
> *But once more again comes*
> *around.*
> *So sleep, my dear, until life*
> *again wakens.*
> *Sleep again, 'til it's found.*
> *Dreams should be had, and never*
> *forsaken.*
> *Sleep 'til the morning*
> *rebounds.*

I couldn't remember the rest of the words
after that. I know that I knew them, but I
was so distraught, they just wouldn't come to

my mind. Then, from somewhere outside my
room, I heard them come back to me, in choked
sobs, and I joined the mysterious voice in the
rest of the song.

> *Tonight, as we hear, the birds
> have stopped   singing.*
> *The crickets now making their
> sound.*
> *To lull us asleep with stars
> above twinkling,*
> *And firelight to help us wind
> down.*
> *So sleep, my love, hold tight
> to your visions,*
> *Cause few things in life are
> profound.*
> *Dreams should be had, and never
> forsaken,*
> *So sleep until justice is
> found.*

I lay there in the darkness for a moment
or two, pondering the voice from outside my
room. The lullaby that we had shared in was
one that I didn't think anybody outside of my
little family had known.

"Who's there?" I called out to the
voice.

"I'm nobody," the voice called back,
"Don't worry about me, you're better off if
you forget about me."

"But that song," I protested. "My mother
said that it was a song that her mother made
up a long time ago. Where did you hear it?"

"That's impossible," the voice answered,
"my mother made that song up to sing to me and
my twin sister. I would like to know where
you heard it."

"What is your sister's name?" I asked, feeling a little chill in my bones.

"Sheena," the voice replied.

"Well," I answered, breathless, "I have some news for you. That's my mother."

The voice went quiet for a moment. I was confused. I never knew that Sheena had a sister. The family that had raised her had all gotten sick and died while she was on a long hunting trip at sixteen. We never really talked about Sheena's family, except for that one conversation that had to do with the song. I had a million questions for this woman, but if I didn't get her talking again, I didn't know if I would ever get them answered.

"Hello?" I called out.

"How did she get away?" the voice answered back.

"I don't know what you are talking about," I replied. "I am just now finding out that Sheena had another family outside of the people in our tribe."

"Tribe?"

"You aren't from a tribe?" I questioned.

"No," the voice said, "we were from the towns."

"Well, then how did you get here, and how did Sheena get into the tribes?" I interrogated.

"Someone's coming," the voice declared urgently, "we can't talk anymore. Trust me, it wouldn't be a good idea."

Then, just like that, the conversation abruptly ended as three or four pairs of feet started to trudge through the hallways outside. I was disappointed by the circumstances. I really wanted to understand what had happened with Sheena and her sister, and why they were separated. I had a feeling that I would find out sooner or later, so I allowed myself to drift off to sleep.

The next morning I was roughly aroused by the king. He seemed very angry about something and for a moment I thought that he might have been listening to the conversation between Sheena's sister and me last night. She seemed to think that talking to me would be a punishable offense, and maybe she was right.

"What were you doing sleeping on the floor?" he asked me fiercely. "Only animals sleep on the floor. From now on you will sleep in the bed, like everyone else around here does." I hastily nodded my agreement.

"You will put these on," the king ordered, thrusting some clothing at me. "Those things that you have on now will be thrown. What you are wearing now isn't appropriate for the castle. Burn it after you have changed." I looked down at my clothing. It was my summer clothing for the forest. I realized how little of my body it actually covered and thought about the clothing that I saw on the women while coming into the king's castle. All you saw of them were their arms and faces. I cringed, thinking about how hot all of that fabric would be, and how hard it would be to climb and hunt while wearing it.

"My shoes!" I pleaded, remembering my secret pocket with my necklace inside it. "I can keep my shoes, can't I?" The king looked down at my shoes with a disgusted look on his face.

"Those shoes are dirty," he argued. "They are heathen shoes. You will throw them away as well." My face fell, and I caught a glint of satisfaction in his eyes.

Then he left and I tried to figure out a way to keep my necklace safe without him finding it. I knew that I couldn't chance disobeying him because he was holding Cub somewhere out of my protection. I was never afraid for myself even once since he had captured us and brought us here. I only wanted to make sure that Cub was never harmed. If it weren't for her, I would have gladly fought him every inch of the way. I might even be dead right now.

I examined the clothing that I was supposed to change into. There wasn't even a slight hint of a pocket in the dress, and the shoes were only slippers. I couldn't sew a patch on anywhere because the fabric was so thin that it would create a bulge anywhere I tried it. I couldn't wear the necklace around my neck for the same reason. I realized that I wouldn't be able to keep my necklace on me, and it was dangerous to keep it in the room. Either way, I was in a bad position.

I put off wearing the clothes the king had given me as long as I could by picking the bedding up off the floor and making the bed. I did the job as slow as I could so if the king returned I could look like I had just been busy tidying up before putting on the new clothes. I hoped that this would give me the time I needed to come up with a plan. It didn't.

I was no closer to figuring out what to do with my necklace when I had no choice but to adorn the new clothing. I carefully disrobed and folded my forest clothing and set them neatly on the bed. Then I put the new clothing on. I sat and stared at my forest clothing, wondering how ridiculous I must look in the strange attire that I had on now.

I began to pace around the room. I was nervous about the necklace, but the thought of losing the last bit of the forest that I held onto horrified me as well. Losing my clothing was like losing any ties that I had to the forest. Now the last string was about to be cut.

Finally, I decided to get it over with. It wouldn't do me any good to put it off any longer. I would just have to place the necklace under the mattress of the bed and hope for the best. I walked toward the bed and then felt myself falling. I had tripped over something. I laid there on the floor, face down for a moment. I didn't want to get back up and do what I had to do. I turned my head so that my cheek was resting against the hard wooden floor and then reached my arms under the bed to spread out a little. My fingers caught on something and I felt a floorboard come loose and slide out of the floor. I had found a hiding place for my necklace.

I lifted up the flap of leather on my boots and quickly grabbed the necklace out of the secret pocket. I threw it into the opening in the floor. Then I realized that it was big enough to hide my clothing as well, so I stuffed that inside too. I replaced the floorboard as quickly as I could and started a fire. I didn't know how long it would be before the king came back so I wanted it to look as if I had burned the clothes.

He had given me a lot more time than I thought he would. I sat and watched as the wood I had put on the fire dwindled down. I think it was probably three hours after he had awakened me before he showed up. He looked around the room for any sign of my clothing and then nodded his head in approval when he couldn't find anything. I breathed a sigh of relief when I saw him check under my mattress for the clothing. It was a good thing I had found the loose floorboard under the bed.

"It's time for breakfast," the king began, "you will serve me. After I have eaten, you will eat with the rest of the servants. That is your new role." I realized that this had been his plan all along. I was going to be forced to wait on the person I hated most for the rest of my life. I contemplated other forms of torture, and found them preferable to this one.

I followed him down to the kitchen, and he introduced me to his other servants. They all seemed cheerful and happy. I came to find out later that I was the only one who was forced into working for him.

The head servant, a man named Garth, began giving me instructions on what to do. He told me to make certain dishes. I explained to him that I had never made them before and he seemed surprised. He called over another servant, Rossannah, to teach me. I would be making these dishes a lot over the next year.

Rossannah was not like the other servants. She was kind to me and didn't ignore me. She was patient. She seemed to understand that the chores of the forest and the chores of a castle are entirely different. Even if she didn't understand the difference, she never let on. She was almost like a forest woman herself. She was rough and outspoken and didn't seem to care about the kind of manners that were so important to the other servants. I asked her what made her that way. She told me that her father used to be a slave and only those who cared about royalty and traditions teach their children *those kinds of manners*. Even though Rossannah didn't really fit in with the others, she seemed to be loved by everyone.

After we had finished making breakfast, Rossannah handed me a big pot of what I now know was oatmeal. She grabbed another pot. A few other servants took the other things that we had made. We all headed out to the dining room. Rossannah told me to watch her so I would know how to serve the king, but as soon as we got out there, my eyes could not see her anymore.

"Cub!" I cried. She was sitting at the table with the king. Her eyes brightened as soon as she saw me and she got up to run to me, but was stopped by the sound of the king's voice.

"Sit down!" he scolded her. "A proper young lady does not speak to the servants. You will not speak to that woman unless you are giving her an order. Do I make myself clear?" The order he had given her came crashing down on me and I felt a painful stab in my heart. I looked at him with pleading eyes, but all he did was give me that evil smile. I looked down at the pot of hot oatmeal that I had in my hands and thought about tossing it in his face. I held back the urge for Cub's sake.

"Serve us!" He ordered. I sighed and then realized I could say something to Cub. I walked over to her and asked if she wanted some oatmeal. She looked up at me and smiled a weak little smile and nodded her head. It was the only communication we were allowed, and we took full advantage of it. I scooped some oatmeal onto her plate and walked to the side that the king was on. I scooped some oatmeal onto his plate as Rossannah came behind me and gave him some of whatever she had. She then took me by the arm, gently, and guided me over to the door where we waited with the dishes in our hands. The other servants finished and came to join us.

We were all left standing there until a woman of about forty appeared. She walked in and stroked the king's hair before sitting down next to him. She peered across the table at Cub and smiled. I instantly did not like her. It was something about the way that she carried herself.

"Good morning," she said to Cub. She gave a little wave of her hand and the servants all went to her side to serve her. She thanked us sweetly and we went back to our places.

"You may go now," the king ordered. We all went back into the kitchen. There was a table in the kitchen where all the servants set the dishes. They sat down in the chairs around the table. Rossannah motioned for me to sit next to her.

"Who was that?" I whispered as I sat down next to her.

"The king's mother," she whispered back, "she's going to be raising and teaching the kid. I guess they are planning on creating a lady or something to marry off to the southern king's son. That is what the rumor is anyway."

"They can't do that!" I raged. The other servants looked at me in disgust. Rossannah held her finger to her lips to warn me to stay quiet.

"Don't worry," Rossannah soothed me, "I'm pretty sure it is just a rumor."

We ate in silence. I disliked the taste
of everything I put in my mouth. I had grown
accustomed to having fresh meat and berries,
or other wild foods and didn't like the grainy
foods that they seemed to eat here.
Everything that they ate was raised.
Everything that I wanted was wild.

After breakfast, Rossannah and I got back
to work. She taught me how to prepare more
food that I had never cooked before. It all
took an extremely lengthy time to prepare.
While waiting for food to cook, we started to
clean up. Then we served the food again.
Then we ate whatever was left over. We did
the same for supper.

When all the meals for the day had been
done, I was told that I could rest until the
morning. I was no longer locked in my room,
but I was told that I could never leave the
castle grounds. I thought about trying to
find Cub and escape, but something told me I
would never find her. Even if I could find
her somehow, there were guards everywhere and
I would never be able to escape with her in
tow. I wandered around the castle, looking
for weak spots that I might use to my
advantage at a time when it would be possible
for me to leave. I didn't find any the first
day. Finally, I became so exhausted, that I
had no choice but to find my way back to my
room and collapse on the bed. I had no
trouble sleeping that night.

Rossannah woke me up the next morning.
She had decided that she was going to take me
under her wing. I appreciated the kindness
from her. I knew that I wasn't going to
receive it from anyone else, and so our
friendship began.

CHAPTER SEVEN

CUB OUTSMARTS THE KING

It took me a long time to get used to my new role. I had never done a lot of cleaning chores before. We lived in the forest. The little cleaning that we had to do was usually reserved for the very old or very young members of the tribe who couldn't hunt, gather, or protect the tribe because they were too weak. When we moved to the cave, the cleaning chores were given to Cub, and Joseph would help out when he was around. Sometimes Sheena would take time to help with dishes, but I never did anything like that. It was new territory for me.

In addition to the unfamiliar chores, I was homesick for the forest. I missed climbing the trees, picking berries, hunting for my food, and the sounds. Sometimes I had trouble falling asleep at night because of the absence of the sounds.

Cub must have been missing home, too. When I saw her at meal times she seemed tired and lonesome. As time went on she seemed to eat less and less. Soon, her face became pallid and worn. The king and his mother tried to encourage her to eat more, but she seemed determined to eat only enough to keep her alive.

The king's mother seemed especially anxious about Cub's condition. I would often hear her discussing Cub in hushed tones with the king when they thought nobody was listening. From their conversations I found out that it was true that they were planning on grooming Cub for marriage. It wasn't the king's original intention for her when he brought her to the castle, but the moment his mother saw her she pronounced Cub to be the perfect candidate. Apparently, it was a custom of the kingdoms to choose girls for the other future kings to promote peace between them. They groomed these girls and when the future king was ready to marry he would choose between them. Usually the kingdom that produced the best girl was rewarded in trade. They got the richest pickings for a very long time. Cub, however, was not being a model student and was losing a lot of her good looks in the process. The king's mother suggested that the king give her a present to encourage her to go along with the training, something that she really wanted.

For the next two weeks I watched as the king showered Cub with gifts. I watched from a distance as he brought her out to ride her very own horse. Cub sat on the horse somberly as the king led her around for an hour, trying in vain to make her smile. Finally, he became frustrated and gently lifted Cub off of the beautiful white horse. He looked down at her, disappointed, and shook his head. He told her to stay where she was while he put the horse back in the stables. He took the horse's reins and led it away, and as soon as he left, I saw Cub's mouth turn upward. I knew then that she had been having a good time, but didn't want the king to know it.

The next day, the castle was flooded with an array of fancy dresses, all for Cub. There were so many dresses of so many different materials and it was impossible to count them all. They kept on arriving, one after the other, and Cub just sat there, eyeing them with disinterest. But I watched her, and once she knew that the king and his mother were looking away, she reached out and stroked one of the soft, silky ones.

One day they offered her toys. Another day they offered her beautiful caged birds. She was even given her own garden to play in and they told her she could order the gardener to plant whatever she wanted in it. Even though I was not able to witness it all, I knew Cub was pretending not to care about any of it. I knew she was secretly admiring her new things behind the king's and his mother's back. Cub was holding out for something, and I was anxious to find out what it was.

"She's really quite clever," Rossannah said to me when we were alone in the kitchen one day. "She'll make an excellent princess. All that nonchalance and underneath it all she's just trying to get more."

"Oh, Cub isn't really like that," I informed her. "But she does have something up her sleeve."

And Cub did have something up her sleeve. It didn't take her long to realize how important she had become to the king's mother, and how important the king's mother was to him. I wasn't going to be left in the dark about her intentions for much longer.

"Please, Cub," the king's mother pleaded with her over breakfast one morning, "Could you eat just a little bit more?" Cub just stared into her eyes, blankly. The king's mother elbowed him to try to encourage Cub.

"Why aren't you happy, Cub?" the king asked, exhausted. "What can we give you to make you happy?"

"Well," Cub spoke softly, "there is one thing I want. It would make me very happy. I might even do better at lessons if you were to give it to me. But I know that you never would."

"What is it?" The king's mother demanded eagerly. "Anything you want is yours."

"Do you promise?" Cub asked, slyly. She glanced over at the king who was peering at her with a curious look on his face.

"You can have anything you want," the king's mother promised, "Except to leave. You have to stay here and take lessons."

"I want Joby!" Cub exclaimed, excitedly. Both the king's and his mother's mouth dropped open instantly. It took them a few moments to recover from the shock.

"Absolutely not!" the king raged. "She is needed in the kitchen."

"But you promised me," Cub whimpered to the king's mother. "You said I could have anything that would make me happy!"

"I did say that," the king's mother agreed. She and the king were locked in a stare down. It only took a few seconds of his mother's scolding gaze before the king relented.

"Oh, fine," he fumed, "but this doesn't mean that she is off the hook for chores. She will have some to do when the little girl goes to bed at night."

"Come sit here, Joby!" Cub chirped. "We can have breakfast together now!" I was frozen in place by shock. I didn't realize how smart Cub really was until that moment. She must have been planning this for a long time.

"Sit down!" the king yelled at me, enraged. "And hand that dish to someone else." I gave the oatmeal that I was holding to one of the other servants and sat down beside Cub. The other servants were ordered to bring me a plate and serve me. I could feel their hatred as each of them scooped food onto my plate. Rossannah winked at me as she came through with her dish. Rossannah made this awkward situation feel okay.

I kept my eyes lowered on my plate as I picked through my food nervously. I could tell that the king was watching me the entire time, plotting how he would make me suffer for this event and others to come. Cub sat beside me, eating as she hadn't done in weeks, blissfully unaware of the tension.

"If I have to eat with her," the king remarked as he left the table, "she will have to learn some manners. She will undergo lessons with the child. Make sure that she is setting a good example for the girl, Mother."

"I agree with you," the king's mother replied, looking at me with repulsion. "She is awful at the table. She is pretty, though. Who knows? She might also come in handy some time down the road. I'll make ladies of them both."

I looked up at Rossannah to try to make sense of what I had heard from the king's mother. Her eyes had gone wide and she had a stricken look about her. I knew at that point that I was in trouble; I just didn't know what kind. I told myself that I would find Rossannah as soon as I was able to find out what was going on.

As breakfast ended, the king's mother announced that we were done and I stood up and began to clear the table out of habit. It was a chore I had become so used to doing that it was almost a reflex.

"Sit down, Joby!" she scolded me crossly. "That is no longer your responsibility. I'm sure you will have other responsibilities, but while you are in my presence, you will not smell like sweat. I have a very sensitive nose and so you will bathe every morning before coming to breakfast now, or after your chores are done at night. In fact, go and bathe right now before lessons."

"Bathe?" I asked, confused. I had not been aware that there was any smell to me at all. When I grew up in the forest, we only bathed when we came to a stream or a lake, but I was never really aware of anybody smelling badly, and I had not seen any water sources around castle grounds. "Where do I bathe?"

"Don't get smart with me," the king's mother said, angrily. "Go to the bathroom and take a bath."

"I'm not sure what you are talking about," I maintained. Rossannah had been listening intently to our conversation as she was clearing the table. She set the dishes she held back on the table.

"I will show her," Rossannah offered, and the king's mother waved us away.

Rossannah led me through the castle to a part where there were many rooms. It was a part that I had not been to yet. She brought me into a room where there was a sink, and some structures I had not seen before.

"This is a bathroom," Rossannah explained to me, "How were you here for so long and not know what this was?"

"I've never had to use it before," I answered.

"What have you been doing with your waste?"

"You know the ash bucket for the fireplace? I use that and then I burn it." I replied. "I didn't know what else to do with it. We bury it in the forests."

"I guess that makes sense," Rossannah agreed, "but don't tell anybody that is what you have been doing. It would sound savage to others who are from this world. Plumbing has been around for a very long time. It's from the old world, before it was destroyed."

"What do you mean the old world?" I asked, intrigued.

"Things weren't always this way," Rossannah explained, "Everything used to be more connected than it is now. But not everybody is going to agree on how to live all the time, so now we have this. That's all I really know about it. The older people seem to know more about it, but a lot of them are even fuzzy on the details. Most of them were only children when the world changed."

Rossannah explained to me how to use the bathroom. I took my bath while she waited outside the door. When I came out she began to lead me back to Cub and the king's mother.

"You shouldn't have to come back to this exact bathroom again. There should be one close to your room. I could wait around for you and help you find one when you are finished with your day." Rossannah offered as we walked along.

"It's nice of you to offer," I said, "but I have a feeling that it is going to be very late before I get back to my room. I can probably manage to find the bathroom myself, now that I know what I am looking for."

"I don't mind waiting for you," Rossannah argued back, "In fact, it would be a lot better than going home to see my father at the end of the night. He's a little crazy. He used to be a slave, a long time ago. He worked in the fields. That is where most of the slaves work. He was pardoned from his debts by the king's father; he and his wife at the time. His wife ended up committing suicide. The older he gets, the more he talks about her now. My father is the reason I work in the castle, as a servant to the king. I dislike him very much, and I am only telling you this because I know that you won't tell anybody. When he started having these tirades about his old wife, he started demanding that we all be appreciative of the king and the fact that he had a son to take over the throne when he passed away. When the old king passed away, he started to pressure me and my siblings to go work for the new king so that we could watch over him. My mother eventually couldn't take it anymore and so she left my father and took my younger brothers, but I stayed behind to take care of him because he just can't take care of himself. He is fine during the day, but at night, he shouts in his sleep. I have to wake him up, but sometimes, I need a rest, too. So I will wait for you tonight."

"I will be glad to provide you with a distraction," I smiled uncomfortably, wondering what I had done to prompt this confession from her. Part of me felt a little out of place, but a bigger part of me felt relieved that I knew a little more about Rossannah than I had before. It gave me a sense of security to know that I was developing a true friendship with someone in this place where I was nothing more than an outsider to so many people. Having Rossannah as a friend could be my ticket to getting out of this place.

We eventually found Cub and the king's mother again. Cub ran up to me and hugged me tight as soon as she saw me. The king's mother also approached me, and circled around me as a hawk would around its prey before it swooped down and clutched it in its razor sharp talons. I imagined her as a hawk from that point on. Rossannah and I even called her that when she wasn't around.

"We will have to get you new clothing for when you are taking lessons with Cub," the Hawk informed me. "Those are servants clothing. You will wear proper clothing when you are with me, you will change into your servant's clothing after. Stand still while I take your measurements." I did what I was told, but that didn't stop her from taking a thin stick and whacking me with it from time to time, claiming that I was fidgeting when I obviously wasn't.

After my measurements were taken, we spent the rest of the day doing things that I found very silly. We spent almost the entire day walking from one end of the room to the other, stopping only for meal times. Every once in a while, the Hawk would stop us and explain to us what we were doing wrong, and then tell us to walk to the other side of the room all over again. She seemed very pleased with Cub's improvements, but became increasingly more agitated with me.

"How old are you?" The Hawk demanded, when she became so flustered she could no longer hold it in.

"Sixteen," I replied.

"I do not see how a sixteen-year-old woman can't get the hang of something as easy as walking, yet a mere six-year-old child gets it within the first day," the Hawk insulted.

I just shrugged my shoulders. I wasn't even trying. I didn't care about any of this.

"I guess it's just not as important to me as it is to you," I said, honestly. "I'm not somebody's pet to be trained."

"Cub," the Hawk fumed, "please, go to supper, we will be along when your sister learns how to walk properly."

Cub left the room, obviously disconcerted. She knew that I had already put myself in a bad situation by mouthing off to the Hawk. Any transgression that she could commit would be quickly forgiven because of her young age and importance, but I would not be so lucky. As soon as Cub was out of the room, the Hawk took out her flimsy little stick and began hitting me with it like it was a whip. It didn't hurt that much, but I knew that if I let her know that, my punishment might become more intense.

When the Hawk finished disciplining me, I did as I was told and paid more attention to my lesson. We headed off to supper ten minutes after that. I decided that I would play her little game for now because I didn't want to be barred from Cub and any chance of finding a way to escape with her.

At supper, the Hawk informed the king of the way that I had acted during lessons. He looked at me with disdain in his eyes and warned me that he would take over punishments if my behavior didn't get better. I nodded my agreement to him, although inside I was planning out every last detail of my escape. I just needed to find the weakness in the castle and the guards that would help me put my plan into action.

After supper, it was Cub's free time. We were both allowed to do what we wanted for an hour before Cub was to be put to bed by the Hawk. Cub wasted no time in showing me where her room was. Apparently, she had been thinking about escaping just as much as I had been. We might have attempted it that night had it not been for the Hawk trailing us everywhere we went.

"Come here, Joby," Cub whispered to me as she brought me to the window in her room. "Look out of this window."

I looked straight down in the direction that Cub was pointing. The castle was made of rock that I could easily climb down, and there was wall right below that separated the outside from the castle grounds. There was about a mile of fields beyond the wall, and then a forest full of beautiful trees. Trees we could hide in if we could make it past the fields.

"Look at my garden," Cub said loudly, for the Hawk's benefit. "Isn't it pretty? We should go into my garden tomorrow."

Cub had already planned out the whole escape while I had only been thinking about it. I was extremely proud of her, but I knew her plan would never work unless we could shake the Hawk.

"I don't know, Cub," I answered her, looking into her eyes and trying to help her read my mind. "That is up to the king and his mother, don't you think? They are in charge."

Cub seemed to understand what I was trying to say to her. She nodded her head and we came away from the window. I looked out at the forest one last time before walking away. I really missed those trees.

When Cub was put to sleep, the Hawk brought me to the king. He explained to me that my new chores would be to clean all of the floors in the castle. I had to do a certain number of rooms every night, and the number of rooms I had to do would depend on my behavior every day. If I was obedient and did as I was told, I would be given only two hours of work, but if I acted up in any way, I would not get to sleep that night. Moreover, I was given a new rule that I could not get my clothing or slippers dirty because with my new schedule, I would more than likely not have the time to wash them. The king and his mother seemed absolutely obsessed with the idea that I should never be dirty anymore.

That night I was given seven large rooms, which took me six hours to clean, because of my attitude with the Hawk earlier. I took off the slippers that I had on and pulled up my dress to my knees to keep my clothes from getting dirty as I swept and mopped the floors. I was happy to find Rossannah waiting for me when I finished the chores.

"Thank you for waiting for me," I smiled at her when she came to get me.

"If I would have been able to find you earlier," she said, "I would have helped you do the rooms. You must be exhausted."

"It's not so bad," I smirked, "they think that they are making it unbearable, but as long as I get to see Cub I'm going to be just fine."

"I'm happy for you," Rossannah warned, "but just watch out. I don't like what the king's mother said about you 'coming in handy'. I've seen girls become concubines because they were pretty. The fact that the king's mother sees potential in you is not necessarily a good thing."

"It's not like they are going to do anything like that while Cub is still around,"

I argued. "They need me to keep her happy, and I don't plan for us to be around long enough for them to marry her off."

"Just be careful," Rossannah said, again. "You never know. I've known these people longer than you have, and they have all the power around here. Nobody stands up to them, short of the people in the forest, and look what happened to them." I stopped walking. That last comment made me feel vulnerable and angry.

"I'm sorry," Rossannah apologized, "I didn't mean it like that."

"I'm going to stand up to them, Rossannah," I vowed. "It might take me a little while, but I am going to stand up to them, and I am going to win."

"I hope so," Rossannah sighed.

Rossannah and I walked around the corridors close to my room until we found the closest bathroom. I decided to bathe right then so that I could sleep a little longer in the morning. I had been drilled by the Hawk before I had been left to my chores that I shouldn't be late for meal times. I intended to do everything I could to show that I was on their side until I could find a way to escape so that they wouldn't become suspicious of me.

The next morning I woke up to find new clothing draped over the foot of my bed. Someone must have put it there in the night and I realized that it was supposed to be the proper clothing that I had to wear for lessons. I put it on and realized that it was much bulkier than the thin servant's clothing that I had been wearing for chores. I flirted with the idea of keeping my necklace in a pocket in the dress, but decided that this would still be a bad idea and that my necklace was safe where it was for the time.

I made it to breakfast on time. The king seemed disappointed when I showed up. I know he was probably hoping that I wouldn't so that he could add more hours to my nightly chores. I sat down and forced myself to smile sweetly at him across the table and say "good morning" as the Hawk had instructed me to do. She seemed awfully pleased with herself when I did it.

"We will go out to the garden today before lessons, as Cub had requested that we do last night," the Hawk announced to us while we were eating. "Fresh air is good for the complexion anyway." My heart jumped. It might be possible to escape today.

"Isn't today a harvest day?" the king asked his mother.

"Yes," the Hawk replied. "There will be hundreds of slaves and their masters on the other side of the wall. We are very fortunate to have very loyal subjects in our kingdom."

I bit my lip. I realized that the Hawk was trying to tell me that she knew that Cub and I were planning to escape and she wanted me to know that she had already thought of that. We wouldn't be able to escape today, and as long as she knew that we had a plan to jump the wall, she could keep us away from it when escape was possible. I underestimated her.

"After the garden," the Hawk continued, "I will begin to teach these girls how to read. It's come to my attention that they have never had any formal education while living in the forests. Neither of them knows how to read a single word."

The garden was beautiful and it felt good to be outside. Cub had requested that some apple trees be planted so that when they grew she could simply reach up and pick fresh apples for herself. They were carefully positioned in the middle of the garden, far away from the wall. They were small, but they gave off a rustling sound when the wind went through them. I enjoyed that sound. I had missed it very much.

After the garden, we were brought back inside. The Hawk handed us each a book. I had never seen one before. It fascinated me. The Hawk was thrilled with my sudden interest in something she was teaching. I tried to act uninterested when I noticed how happy it made her, but I couldn't keep up the charade. I was instantly caught up in the world of books from that first day when she started us on the alphabet. I looked forward to learning how to read every third day as much as I despised all of the other stuff that she taught us. After a year, I could read as well as she could.

CHAPTER EIGHT

OUR ESCAPE

I stopped resisting the Hawk completely at some point in my training, even though I could tell that Cub still was. It wasn't that I didn't want to get away. I had just become comfortable with the schedule I was on.

Sometimes at night I would still lie awake and think about ways to escape, but I had stopped trying to actively find a way out of the castle. I thought that eventually, an opportunity would present itself and I would be able to leave with Cub.

The work that I had to do was never really as hard as when I was in the forest, except for when I let my mouth get the better of me and was forced to be up all night cleaning the floors. The cleaning wasn't the hard part; it was the sleep deprivation that got to me. It made it hard to focus on the things that I knew that I should be focusing on. The long nights were becoming less and less, though.

Eventually, I was rewarded with a little more trust from the Hawk. She would let me go out into the garden by myself from time to time, although never with Cub. She always kept Cub in her sights. I usually went out into the garden on the days that Cub was given reading lessons. She wasn't picking reading up as easily as I had, which the Hawk said was normal for a child her age.

While I was out in the garden I would inspect the wall. It would be easy to climb, but that wasn't the problem. There were always people on the other side now. It had been ordered by the king. The Hawk must have talked to him.

One day while I was in the garden alone, Cub came running out by herself. She begged me to put her on her back and climb over the wall. I thought about it for a moment and then told her it would be a bad idea because we would never get past the fields. From out of nowhere, the Hawk appeared and congratulated me on a job well done. Apparently, she had allowed Cub to slip away from her to see what would happen if she let her come to me. She informed me that I would be allowed to bring Cub out to the garden from then on, because I finally understood that I could never get away.

"I miss home, Joby," Cub would tell me every time we were in the garden alone. "Let's just try to get away."

"I will find a way out for us," I would tell her. "This is not the way. Even if we do get over the wall, I could not get us across the fields in time. If I were alone, I could make it, but you are too small and will slow me down. When you get bigger, we will both be able to go fast enough to get away. Just keep exercising like I told you to make those muscles fast." Then I would watch her as she would sprint through the garden, trying to make herself faster. It hurt me to tell her "no" but I didn't have a choice. As long as I could get her away before she was old enough to be married, it didn't matter that I was caged for a while.

Then something else changed that would force me to speed up my plans for escape. After two years of captivity, the Hawk seemed to become as obsessed with my progress in training as she had been with Cub's.

One night I was told that I would stop doing the chores I had been doing for two years, except for one night a week. I was forced to do extra training when Cub was put to bed at night in place of those chores. It wasn't hard to figure out that they had the same kind of plans for me as they had for Cub.

I learned from Rossannah, who had been spying on the Hawk and the king for me whenever she got the chance that the southern king's wife had died during childbirth. He was now looking for a new wife that wasn't "as delicate" as his last wife. The Hawk figured that they had an advantage because the other kingdoms had not been training girls, but they had me training for two years already. She further surmised that if the southern king chose to take me on as his bride, that Cub would be pushed to work harder on her training so that she would be chosen by the southern king's son and we could eventually be together again.

I was crushed by the news. I thought that I would be able to get Cub out before either of us had to worry about the Hawk and the king using us for their own selfish gains. Now it seemed that I would have to escape on my own and try to come back for Cub later, or accept that I was in a no win situation and pray that the southern king wouldn't take an interest in me.

I decided in the end that I could not leave Cub alone. It might be easier to wait to see if she was chosen by the southern king's son and escape when she came to join me there. They probably wouldn't expect us to be so rebellious if we acted like we truly wanted to be chosen by them.

When Cub and I were in the garden alone, I told her what Rossannah had told me about the Hawk's new plans for me. Then I told her to be on her best behavior when the southern king came as I had learned that he was already on his way to see me. If my plan worked, it might be years before we could see each other again, but it was our only real chance for getting out.

The Hawk and the king did not say anything to us about the impending visit from the southern king. There was no preparing us for the possibility that we would soon be ripped apart. I think the Hawk figured that if we knew, we would act out and try everything in our power to not be picked by the southern king.

Then one day, he showed up. He was a man in his thirties. He seemed kind, which I hadn't expected. I felt like I might be able to care for him if I wasn't being forced into the situation. I had mixed feelings. I knew that I had to act as if I didn't know why he was there, and utilize everything that I had been taught by the Hawk. Still, something in me wanted to break down and be rude and lash out at him and my captors. Then I felt guilt for feeling that way about such a nice man.

The southern king had also brought his son. Cub seemed to take a liking to him right away. However, she had instantly forgotten her manners and she ran off with the prince, playing rough games and screaming at the top of her lungs. The southern king seemed to find these things endearing and laughed as he watched Cub wrestle the prince (who was four years older than her) to the floor.

I looked over at the Hawk as she was watching the children in disgust. She seemed to involuntarily flinch every few seconds. I was very amused by this and couldn't keep my eyes off the spectacle.

"She's very serious, isn't she?" The southern king chuckled softly, leaning in close to me so that the Hawk could not hear anything he said.

"You have no idea," I whispered back, smiling at him. I thought to myself that maybe it wouldn't be such a bad thing to get stuck with this man for the next few years while I waiting for Cub to come back to me.

"Maybe it would be a good thing to get you girls away from here, so you can have a little fun once in a while?" My heart jumped. My plan was going to work.

"I think you might be right," I replied to him.

The southern king stood up and walked over to where the Hawk was standing and asked to talk to the king. The Hawk smiled sweetly and nodded enthusiastically, then looked at me approvingly. It was the only time I ever got that look from her and it made me sick.

The Hawk led the southern king away, leaving me alone with the two children. The prince pushed Cub away from him and came to sit next to me.

"You are not much older than I am, I bet," he fished. "Probably only a few years difference."

"I'm eighteen now," I remarked back. I started to get uncomfortable.

"You know my father is thinking about marrying you, right?" The prince started again. "So you will be my new mother, and then I will marry Cub."

"I don't think we would have to think of me as your mother," I answered back. "We could just be friends."

"No," the prince insisted. "I think I would like to have another mother. I miss my mother. And besides, it would be strange to have a little sister or brother and have them call you mother. I would have to explain to them why I don't call you mother."

Then I realized I had not completely thought my plan through and I became very nervous. There was one thing that had not entered my mind: sex. It dawned on me that going through with this plan meant years of having a sexual relationship with someone that I did not care for, and possibly becoming pregnant with an unwanted child as a result. If that happened, escape would be much more complicated.

Along with the likelihood of pregnancy, I was worried about the overall experience of sex. I knew about sex, of course, but I had never had it. Even though Joseph and I had been together, we had never come close to sharing that part of a relationship because the close quarters of the cave allowed us no privacy. I did not want my first time to happen because I was trying to keep up with a charade that I had constructed to carry Cub and me to freedom.

I thought about doing something to destroy the progress I had made with the plan, but then I remembered that this was not just my life I was playing with. There was not another way that I could safely get Cub and myself out of this horrible situation. I decided again to go through with it.

That night, the southern king and the prince left to go back home. Cub and I were informed the next morning at breakfast that I was going to be his new wife. We acted as though we were distraught by the news, although we were jumping for joy inside. We argued with the king and the Hawk profusely. Cub even threw herself on the floor and acted out a very convincing tantrum, screaming that she would no longer take part in training. The Hawk picked her up and sat her back down on her chair firmly. Cub pouted and crossed her arms. I was very amused by the whole scene but was careful not to show it.

"There's more," the Hawk announced, once we had settled down. "The southern king says that he wants to take Cub as well for his son once she is old enough, but there is a stipulation."

"What?" I asked, surprised.

"He wants her to go to a school, right now," the Hawk grumbled, annoyed. "He doesn't want me doing her training anymore."

"What kind of school?" I asked, alarmed. I was nervous about any change in the plan because sometimes changes bring unknown obstacles. If she remained with the Hawk I knew that I would have Rossannah here to watch over her.

"It's a school for young ladies," the Hawk answered me, clearing her throat. "It's in the southern kingdom. The prince would be able to visit her there whenever he wants. It's very remote, and very well guarded."

I looked down at my plate. It was good that Cub would be closer to me than I originally thought. However, that wouldn't help me escape with her if I couldn't find the school, or get Cub out of it.

"The southern king is sending someone for Cub tomorrow," the king said abruptly, wanting to end the conversation. "He will come for you next month."

"Wait!" I responded, alarmed. "Tomorrow? That's not enough time to say goodbye. I thought we would have more time."

"It's going to have to be enough," the Hawk said tersely. "We don't want to hear another word about it."

I silenced myself. I knew it was not worth it to try to start an argument now. Still, it was going to be unbearable to be stuck here without Cub. I had to remind myself many times that I would see her again in a better situation which we could escape so much easier.

I met up with Rossannah after breakfast to discuss what was happening and to tell her about my escape plan. She seemed upset when I told her that I was going to be married to the southern king, even though I told her it was exactly what I wanted.

"When you hear about my escape," I stated excitedly, trying to cheer her up, "you come into the forest and look for me, and I will eventually find you. You can come live in the forest with my tribe!"

"I just didn't know that you were going too," she sighed, crestfallen, "I knew Cub was going to be sent off to school. I heard the two kings talking about it. The southern king said he didn't want the Hawk teaching Cub anymore because he didn't want Cub to become as frigid as she was. They must have spoken about you before that."

I began to laugh uncontrollably as I imagined the southern king telling the king that his mother was frigid. Rossannah looked at me, confused, but then she realized what she had just said and we both collapsed on the floor in a fit of giggles.

"I'm going to miss you," Rossannah breathed through her laughter, "I don't know of anybody that I care about as much as I care for you."

"If I didn't have to take care of Cub," I smiled, sadly, "I would go to the garden right now and jump the wall, and then you could join me in the forest."

"That would be nice," Rossannah agreed.

"Joby!" Cub appeared, running up to me. "I have a great idea. We can escape tomorrow and never be apart!"

"Shhh," I hushed Cub urgently. "What are you talking about?" Rossannah and I leaned in close so that Cub could whisper to us.

"Remember how you said that I was too slow, and that the southern king and prince wouldn't expect us to try to escape?" Cub said, excitedly. "Well, we are going right through the forests on the way to the school they want to bring me to. I know I am pretty young, but I remember a lot about the forest and how to navigate it. I'll watch where I am going and when we get pretty far away in a thick part of the trees I can tell whoever they have sent for me that I have to go to the bathroom. They won't think twice about giving me a little privacy and when I walk into the forest, they will never find me again. I will head back here to the part of the forest that I can see outside of my bedroom window. I will hang a red scarf in the trees so you know that I have gotten away and then try to find Sheena. Then you can escape from here because you aren't too slow to get away."

"That is a good plan, Cub," I agreed. "And if you manage to get away I will follow you into the woods. Just remember to keep yourself up in the trees once you get a chance to climb one. From my experience, they never look up."

So we had a new plan, thought up by the increasingly more intelligent Cub. I remember at one point I was that smart, but the forest had been taken out of me. I became a little jealous of Cub then. She never had, and never would be stripped completely of the forest.

The next morning came and Cub was shuffled around frantically by the Hawk. She was bathed and dressed and fed while her things were being packed and stacked close to the entrance of the castle, ready to go. I stared at the piles intently, praying that it was the last time Cub would ever see most if not all of those things inside the cases. I was nervous that the plan would fall through and we would be found out and punished for our misdeeds.

Cub and I made a good show of her leaving. We cried and held onto each other and had to be pulled apart. Most of it was an act, but there was a little part of it that was real for us. The hope that everything would work out was stifled a little by a very small pinch of doubt.

"Time for lessons," the Hawk announced to me as Cub climbed into the carriage and was taken away.

"I can't today," I whispered, sadly, allowing a tear to fall from my face. "I feel empty."

"Today I will allow it," the Hawk sighed, showing an uncharacteristic bit of mercy. "But tomorrow we are back to training." I nodded in agreement.

"I think I will just go up and sit in her room for a while," I sighed heavily. I turned away quickly to hide my smile.

"I think I will go with you," the Hawk glared at me suspiciously. I tried not to show alarm. Maybe she had overheard us talking and knew what we were up to.

She followed me to Cub's room. I sat myself down by the window. I knew that it would be a while before Cub would be able to escape, but I wanted to be there the second that she mounted the scarf in the trees.

I sat and waited at the window until nightfall, while the Hawk watched me. I began to get nervous when I could no longer see the tree line in the darkness. I wondered if Cub had ever escaped, or if she had been found out. I thought she should have been able to make her way back by now. Maybe she had exaggerated about her ability to find her way through the forests. Maybe she had just gotten scared and changed her mind. I could no longer see the trees, so I decided to go to bed and check them again in the morning.

When the morning came, I quickly made my way to Cub's room again without bringing attention to myself. I scanned the trees for any sign of red. Once again, there was not a trace of red.

I went to breakfast. It was unbearable to sit there with the Hawk and the king without Cub. I felt out of place and lonely. Not even Rossannah's presence and warmth could make me feel at ease.

Then I had my training. It was like a crash course of everything that I had learned. There were a few new things thrown in pertaining to how I should act in a marriage, and the duties of a queen, which I was soon to

be. I was irritated with the implied
responsibilities that I would have that came
along with my new station in life, mostly
because I didn't know yet if Cub had escaped
and paved the way for my own flight.

I checked in the trees for the red scarf
again that night. It still wasn't there. I
began to accept the fact that we would have to
return to the original plan. Cub was
obviously not able to get away. Rossannah
came to comfort me that night. We talked a
little about the forest and she said she would
like to go there one day. It gave me a little
hope. I promised to write to her while I was
in the southern kingdom, even though she
couldn't read.

I checked the trees for three nights.
Nothing ever appeared. I lost all hope and
decided not to drive myself crazy every night
looking for something that was never going to
appear. I began to focus a little harder on
the things I was being taught by the Hawk. I
might not agree with them, but at least it
gave me something to do instead of pity
myself.

Then during breakfast on the fourth
morning that Cub had been gone, a messenger
came. He explained that Cub had gone missing
a day ago and they couldn't find her. They
had looked everywhere for her. The king
immediately sent some of his own men out to
the forests nearest to his castle. They were
told to watch for her because she would
probably come back to alert me. Then I was
locked in my room.

The Hawk came to my room every day with
my meals and to teach me. Even though it was
well known that I would probably try to
escape, she wanted to make sure that I knew

that they weren't going to give up on me being their bargaining chip. I did as I was told, always looking for an opportunity to get away when they weren't looking, but I was guarded night and day.

I figured that Cub would be smart enough to figure out that she couldn't send me a sign without getting caught, or at least I hoped she was. The best thing for Cub to do would be to forget about me and save herself. I would eventually figure out how to get out.

Then one night while I was sleeping, I was roused awake by hands shaking me gently. I opened my eyes to see Rossannah hovering above me. I opened my mouth to ask her what she was doing there, but she held her finger to her mouth so I would stay quiet. She quickly pulled me out of bed and I knew that she had somehow managed to pave the way for an escape for me.

I pushed the bed away as quietly as I could and pulled the floor boards up to put on my forest clothing and hid the necklace in its old place. The sweet smell of the leather filled my nostrils and I smiled and ran my hands over it.

We left my room and I noticed that the guard who had been assigned to sit at my door for the night was lying on the ground, unconscious. I looked at Rossannah, surprised, wondering how she had managed to put the big man to sleep. She gave me a smile that promised she would tell me later.

Rossannah took me around the corner where there was a basket full of dirty clothing. She pointed to it without saying a word and I knew that she wanted me to climb in. I did and then she covered me with the foul smelling cloth. Then I felt myself being lifted. I wondered who it was that was carrying me. It couldn't have been Rossannah. She was a servant woman, of course, but her features were still so delicate I couldn't imagine her having the strength to lift me.

I was in the basket for about ten minutes before I felt myself being set down. Then all of the cloth was pulled off me and in place of the stench of dirty laundry I could smell the musty smell of hay all around. I sat up and looked around.

"Where am I?" I asked, looking at all of the animals around me.

"My family's barn," Rossannah replied. "It's not safe to go to the forest yet, but I thought I better get you out of the castle at the very least. I think that when the king finds you gone he will pull all the men out of the forests to search the castle for you. And since he thinks there is no way you could possibly get out of the castle because everybody is in the forest, and that you really have nowhere to go, he will have them all search the castle for you."

"What did you do to the guard?" I asked.

"I didn't do anything to him," Rossannah laughed, "except wait for him to pass out himself. I've known that guard for a very long time, and I know that he has a problem with drinking. When I heard he was assigned guard duty, I knew that was my chance to get you out."

"It's a good thing you did before the southern king came back for me," I grinned. "There wasn't a lot of time left."

"Tomorrow we will figure out a way to get you past the fields." Rossannah said, changing the subject. "I'm thinking that if I pull a little cart of my belongings out there nobody would think anything of it. If people stop me I could tell them that I am going to live with my mother. I could hide you under clothing and blankets."

"That sounds like a plan," I agreed, "but are you sure you want to do this. I don't see you ever being able to come back here if we manage to get away."

"I'm not worried about it," Rossannah responded. "My father ran off last night, I have nothing holding me here anymore. And the only person I care about is you, and you are leaving. I want to be with you."

I felt my face turn red. It felt good to hear that I meant so much to Rossannah and I looked forward to having her be a part of my family, but there was still something about her comment and sincerity that made me feel embarrassed. I think it was because I was so unaccustomed to emotional tenderness.

The next morning we followed through with the plan that Rossannah had formed. As I felt the jostling of the cart as it hit each little bump in the fields, I cursed myself for being such a coward and not jumping out and running the fields myself. I realized, however, that I would not only be putting myself in jeopardy, but Rossannah as well. She was risking her life for me and the least I could do was be patient and cautious.

I felt the difference in the way the cart moved as soon as we hit the forest line. Then I could hear the rustling of the leaves again and felt the urge to shout out for joy. I quickly reminded myself to wait until Rossannah gave me the okay.

Half an hour went by and then the cart finally stopped. I knew at this point that it was safe to get out. I threw cloth off of my

body and jumped out of the cart. I breathed
in the forest air and dropped to my knees to
kiss the ground. I scooped up a handful of
dirt and let it run through my fingers back
down to the ground.

Then I turned to Rossannah. I grabbed
both of her hands and began dancing around in
a circle with her. We both laughed like
little children as we spun around and began to
sing songs of nonsense.

Then we heard men's voices shout out to
us. We turned around and saw some of the
king's men, running after us, telling us to
stay where we were. They must have followed
Rossannah the entire way. I grabbed
Rossannah's hand and we began to run.

I dragged Rossannah through the forest as
fast as I could. I tried to make us vanish,
but Rossannah kept stumbling and slowing us
down so that the men were catching up little
by little. I realized that the problem was
Rossannah's dress. It was long and kept
tripping her or getting caught on tree
branches. I knew that if I didn't do
something that we would never get away which
scared me because even though I was still
needed, Rossannah had no use except as a
servant. I shuddered to think of what would
become of her if we were to be caught.

"Hold still," I ordered, stopping for a
short moment. Rossannah didn't move as I
reached down and ripped her dress off of her
body. Now all she had on was underclothing
and would be able to run through the forest
faster.

I grabbed Rossannah again and we went
deeper and deeper into the forest, where the
trees became thicker. The men were falling
farther behind because they seemed to have the

same problem with their clothing that Rossannah had with hers. Soon, I was satisfied with the distance between us.

"Grab the branch of that tree," I commanded Rossannah hurriedly when I thought the men couldn't see us anymore. Rossannah reached up and I pushed her up so that she could swing her body onto the branch. I directed her to keep climbing and hoisted myself up behind her. We stopped and stayed completely silent when we were far up in the trees and hidden by leaves. A moment later we saw the men staggering past the tree we were in and we both breathed a sigh of relief because we knew that we were safe as the bounded past it.

"We'll stay here until we either see or hear them come back around this way." I whispered to Rossannah. "They'll eventually give up trying to find us and then we can go and find Cub and then hopefully find my mother, Sheena."

Rossannah nodded her head in agreement and we sat in that tree for two or three hours while waiting for the men to come back. They finally did and I climbed out of the tree when I could no longer hear their voices. I instructed Rossannah to stay in the tree for a few moments while I looked around and listened for any sign of the men being close by. Then I allowed her to come down as well and we began to walk deeper into the forest.

We looked through the forest for two days before coming into a clearing inhabited by a tribe. I walked up to one of the women and told her my name and asked if she had seen a little girl that looked like Cub. The woman told me to wait and she would go and get the Grandmother of the tribe. I sighed when I

heard the term and thought back to
Grandmother. The woman smiled at me and
walked off toward one of the caravans.

Rossannah and I sat down by a fire with
our backs turned toward the caravans. We were
both exhausted from lack of sleep and neither
of us had had very much to eat.

"Joby!" I heard a familiar voice cry and
I turned around to find Sheena running toward
me from the caravans. I immediately started
to cry and stood up to run to her.

Behind Sheena a tiny figure came bounding
out of the caravan. It was Cub. I shrieked
her name and opened my arms to accept both
Sheena and Cub into them. Sheena kissed my
cheeks and forehead repeatedly, and Cub
wrapped herself around my waist and wouldn't
let go.

After a while, we finally all let go of
each other and I looked down at Cub to realize
that she had been dressed in forest clothing.
Then I remembered that I had ripped
Rossannah's clothing off of her and mentioned
to Sheena that she needed to be dressed.
Sheena took Rossannah off to her caravan and
borrowed her some of her own clothing. I
remember thinking that Rossannah looked like
she belonged in them when they came back.

Then we sat down and talked about what
had happened in the two years that we had been
gone. The tribes had all formed new groups
and Sheena had become the Grandmother of this
one. I looked at Sheena and thought that she
was not old enough to be a Grandmother to a
tribe, but as I looked around, she seemed to
be the oldest one there. It made me feel a
little sad.

Cub apologized for not going through with
the plan. Apparently she had run into Sheena

on her way back to me, and Sheena would not
allow her to leave. Sheena was one person
that you listen to no matter what. I was
grateful for that because Cub and I might
never have made it back to the forest if
Sheena had not stepped in and protected her.

That night I fell asleep listening to all
of the sounds of the forest that I had missed
for so long. I slept on the hard ground next
to the fire, with Rossannah and Cub both lying
on either side of me.

Rossannah would toss and turn: a sign of
someone who had slept in a bed her whole life.
I felt a little guilty for dragging her into
this mess, but I was so happy that it didn't
get to me too much. I was finally home.

CHAPTER NINE

WE MAKE ANOTHER STAND

Rossannah eventually got used to living in the forest, although it was clear that she would never fully fit in with the tribe. One or two of the people of the tribe attempted to teach her to hunt and forage, but ultimately gave up because Rossannah was just no good at things like that. She contented herself with washing the dishes and other small tasks around the clearing that were similar to what she had done before. Many of the tribe members liked her simply because she did the things that were boring to everybody else, but they still had a hard time having a conversation with her.

Rossannah's body became hard and weathered from being exposed to all of the elements, just like the rest of us. She looked more like us every day. She began to smell like the campfire just like we did as well. She mentioned once or twice that she enjoyed that smell and I agreed that it was one of my favorite smells too. She spent a lot more time at the fires than I did, so she was always covered with the scent.

Cub slept inside of a caravan with Sheena. Rossannah and I slept by the fire every night unless it was raining or especially cold. It was still summer, so we were able to sleep outside most nights. Sometimes, the bugs would bother us, but I preferred to live with the little annoyances than to be cooped up in the caravan because I felt as if I had been kept a prisoner inside for too long. I just wanted constant freedom. I think Rossannah slept outside because that is where I was.

A couple of times, Cub and I would bring Rossannah into the woods with us. There we could talk about things that others in the tribe would not understand, which was mainly my obedience to the king for the last two years. The others in the tribe had this idea that I had fought him during my captivity and looked upon me as some sort of hero. This view of me made me feel guilty of how I had actually dealt with my imprisonment and I regretted not being the person that they all saw in me. I let them think what they wanted, for the sake of keeping hope alive inside of them, but it weighed on me every day. Cub and Rossannah were the only ones that I could talk to about it because they were right there with me.

"Sometimes the smartest thing you can do is hold back until you have a weapon or a way to defend yourself," Rossannah reassured me whenever I brought up the subject. "Who knows what would have happened if you fought him. Now you are both back safe in your tribe and I get to be here with you. I am lucky. If you would have fought him, I would still be serving him his meals."

The way that Rossannah laid it out made me feel extremely proud of myself. She always had a way of making me feel that I saved her as well.

It took two or three months before the king caught up with our tribe. Rossannah, Cub, and I were in the woods picking raspberries. Rossannah really liked this chore because she never really got to taste anything fresh before. We always brought her along because we knew how much she liked to pop the raspberries right into her mouth as she picked them.

We weren't far from the tribe when we heard the men yelling from the clearing. I told Cub and Rossannah to stay where they were and got close enough to peer through the trees and see what was happening without exposing myself at the same time. The men who were yelling were the king's soldiers, and the king was there on horseback. He wasn't saying a word. He wasn't barking orders at them. He was just directing his horse silently around the clearing, trying not to miss anything with his eyes.

The men were lining everybody up. It reminded me of when his father had lined all of us up so long ago. When the tribe was all there, he dismounted his horse and walked slowly from one end of the line to the other, sizing them up.

"Is everybody from the tribe here?" he asked. The man that he was standing in front of began to open his mouth.

"Yes," Sheena cut in abruptly, before the man could answer. "This is everybody."

"Don't I know you from somewhere?" The king approached Sheena. "You look very familiar, in more than one way."

"I should look familiar," Sheena said, bitterly. "You took my daughter and her sister from me two years ago."

"Are they not here?" The king perked up, a little too enthusiastically.

"They are not with you?" Sheena asked, shocked. I giggled a little. "I have not seen them in two years."

The king peered into Sheena's eyes. I could tell that he did not trust her.

"Search the forest around this clearing."
The king ordered his men. "If you find Joby,
Cub, or even Rossannah, the tribe will be
killed for hiding fugitives."

I backed away from the clearing and then
ran to the place that I had left Cub and
Rossannah when I knew I was out of sight and
any movement of foliage around me wouldn't be
noticed. I panicked slightly when I could not
find them but breathed a sigh of relief after
hearing Rossannah call to me from above.

"We heard, Joby," Rossannah hissed. "Get
up here."

I laughed to myself as I climbed up into
the trees. I had forgotten that Rossannah's
survival instincts were starting to strengthen
and that she could now climb with little or no
help. I got up to where they were and gave
her a warm nod of approval and then we
silently watched as the men came bounding
through the woods.

We couldn't see them that well this time.
We were in a thick patch of evergreen trees.
It is a little harder to see through them than
other trees. We could hear them talking
though, and we could also hear sounds coming
from the clearing as well. At first, they
sounded optimistic, and then they seemed to
become more frustrated, but they didn't act
like they were going to give up anytime soon.

We were in that tree throughout that
night and halfway through the next day.
Rossannah and I took turns holding Cub when we
realized that she was involuntarily falling
asleep. We settled ourselves on sturdier
branches a little farther down, confident that
we wouldn't be seen because of the thickness.

Eventually, they did leave again. The
king told the tribe that if we ever came to

them, they were to turn us in, or the consequences would be fatal to all of them. We heard everything they said. We heard the tribe agree to it, knowing that they were all lying and risking their lives to make sure that we were safe from him. Then the king and his men left.

We waited for an hour before we came down to make sure that they were not watching the tribe to see if we would come to them. Most of the tribe stayed within the clearing during this period and went about their daily routine, but a select few, led by Sheena, were searching for us through the trees. They passed through, looking up all the time of course, and Sheena was the one who caught sight of us. I immediately brought my finger to my lips to indicate that she shouldn't call out my name. She nodded and motioned for the others to follow her back to the clearing. As a second thought she took her bow and shot an arrow up into a random tree. There was a rustling as a bird fell out of the tree at her feet. She picked it up as if she was looking for a meal the whole time and proudly stuffed it into her sack. Then the search party went back to the clearing.

When we felt that we would be safe, we climbed out of the tree and cautiously reentered the clearing. The other members of the tribe stared as us, nervously. Everyone's eyes darted around the trees, looking for any sign of the king and his men. When night came, we sent the children to bed and sat around the fire, discussing our options.

It was no secret that Cub, Rossannah, and I were all dangerous to the tribe. Therefore, we had to figure out a way to be absent whenever the king and his men were close.

There was no way to know that, however, so the only other option would be for us to stay out of the clearings altogether. We would still hunt and forage for the tribe, and the tribe would bring us supplies that we needed as well. They would cook our food and bring it into the trees for us. However, that didn't solve the problem of what we would do when it got cold, or how we would be protected from the wild animals. Somebody suggested that we build beds in the trees, but that would be too dangerous. The tribe began to squabble about our fate, and I couldn't take it anymore.

"Give me up," I said, when I had heard enough. "I'm the only one he really wants anyway. If you give me up, maybe you can negotiate for the other two."

"That's too risky," Sheena disagreed. "The tribe would be safe, but we don't know what would happen to you three."

"You're right," I conceded, but I still felt that the answer was to drop me at his feet. "Give me tonight to think about this. I know I have the answer, I just need to think about it a little."

The next morning, I approached Sheena with a new plan. I had thought about it that night, and realized that in order to eliminate the constant threat of being discovered; we had to eliminate the person who was posing the threat.

"Think about it, Sheena," I explained, "he has no heir. There is nobody around to take his place and punish us if we were to figure out a way to kill him, and I think that I might know how. We have to ambush him, like he did us two years ago. He's not prepared for it. Let's get the tribes together and I will explain my plan to them."

Sheena sent out the word that we were going to take another stand against the king. It took about two weeks but every tribe that was left after the war was united in our one little clearing. The adults sat around the fire as I explained my plan to them all.

"It centers on giving me up," I began and there was an immediate outcry of dissent among the tribe. I held my hands up to settle the noise and show that I had more to say.

"You won't really be giving me up," I explained. "You will be lulling them into a false sense of security, as if you were now on their side. The king did not seem to have too many men with him. I think that there are more of us. The trick is to get them all out into the open, including the king, and then we kill them all. We leave no witnesses. Nobody will ever know what has become of them, and we will be safe. We will not have to worry about revenge, because he has no close living relatives that I know of besides his mother, and she really cannot do much of anything."

"What if something goes wrong?" Sheena stood up. She took my head in her hands and looked into my eyes as tears began to form. "I just got you back."

"If this works, you will never lose me again," I reassured her.

The plan was voted on by all the members of the tribes and it was decided that we would try it. The only person who voted against it was Sheena. She sulked away to the caravans that night, looking sullen and defeated.

Rossannah and I lay down by the fire that night and talked about the possibility that I might never return. She tried not to act concerned, but I knew by the sound of her voice that she was also feeling distraught about this new course of action that I would be taking.

"If I thought there was any other way," I whispered to her, "I would be taking it."

She reached out her hand and put it on my cheek and I did the same to her. She sighed heavily and we just watched each other for a while. The she rolled over and acted as if she was asleep. I decided to follow suit and pretend to go to sleep as well. When she thought that I was sleeping, she began to sob. I wanted to comfort her, but I knew that she did not want me to know that she was crying, so I just continued to pretend to be away somewhere in dreamland. Inside, however, I was dying.

The next morning, Sheena and I chose the two who would deliver me to the king. We decided on strong, young men who looked as if they would be able to handle me without a problem. For extra assurance, we had them hang on to my arms while I tried to wriggle out of their grasps and get away. We decided that it would be easy to put on a good show with these two hanging on to me.

I said my goodbyes quickly, especially to Rossannah who I sensed would break down if I dragged it out. I told myself that it wouldn't be long before I was back in the tribe again, so a long goodbye would be sending a bad message. I needed to keep up morale for everybody's sake.

Then, my "captors" and I were off to try and find the king and his men. We were followed by the tribes, but at a distance so that we weren't an obvious trap. We weren't even within shouting distance of each other. We figured that while the two men who brought me to the king discussed their reward with him, the tribes could close in and attack while nobody expected it.

It only took us a day to find them. The king and his men were always completely clueless as to how to hide the traces of their trails. I was brought forward, kicking and screaming the whole way. At first, I was acting, but as I got close to that evil, but somehow attractive sneer, my fear kicked in and I found myself truly trying to wriggle myself free and run in the other direction.

"Where is the other two?" The king demanded when I was placed right in front of him. I spit in his face and felt myself swell with satisfaction as he wiped it off with his sleeve.

"Answer me!" He yelled, angrily. Then he slapped me. I opened my mouth in shock. In the two years that I had been his prisoner, he had never hit me once.

"Th-they are safely hid," I managed to stammer out. "I'll never tell you." My cheek hurt. I couldn't get over my confusion at what had just happened to me. I don't know why I didn't expect it, he had hit me before, but he seemed to like to torture me in other ways rather than resort to physical violence.

"Put her down and leave," the king ordered the two men holding me.

"Do we get a reward?" The bigger man asked him.

"Your reward is that I will not kill your tribe," the king said coldly, "Go."

They pushed me to the ground and left. It didn't matter because they would double back and bring the tribes back to rescue me within an hour or less. I would probably have to withstand a bit of torture until then, but I knew that it would be the last that I would feel at his hand, so it didn't bother me too much. Besides, I knew that if he was busy providing me with punishment, he wouldn't see them coming.

He strapped me to a chair, as he had done when he had captured me the first time. I knew that he did this to keep me from fighting back. He was probably stronger than I was, but he was a coward that didn't want any resistance from his victims. Then he just let his hands fly at me, one after the other. I tasted my blood, but it tasted sweet to me. It was almost satisfying. I knew he would never be able to hurt me again after this, and I welcomed every last contact of his palms across my cheeks.

He would stop every few minutes and rest. He would pace back and forth. Sometimes he would call for someone to bring him water or food. He would sit down and enjoy it while watching my blood drip from my nose onto the ground.

Time seemed to drag on, and then it got dark. I lifted my head to look around the forests for some sign of the tribes. Then he would begin to beat me again. It took me a little while to realize that they weren't coming after all. I hung my head, defeated, wondering why they did not come for me. Then he called out for a whip.

"No more!" I cried out, exhausted and torn. "Please, you've made your point."

"No whip," he commanded, waving away his men. "There's no more fight left in her. I can kill her now."

The fear rose up in me when I heard these words. I knew that my chances for survival were slim. I let the men untie me and I fell off the chair onto the ground, waiting for some sort of pain to tear through me that would signal the end of all the pain that I would ever feel. I looked up to see the king, carefully fingering a multitude of weapons, deciding which one would bring about my end. I looked around me and noticed that if I ran I still had a chance to get away alive. There was not even one man close enough to me who would be able to grab me without having to chase me a little first.

I decided that I would run for it. I took a deep breath and jumped to my feet. I ran away from the king as fast as I could. I heard him screaming at his men behind me. I heard footsteps running after me. Then I felt them take me down. They were holding me down on the ground. Two of them had me pinned by my arms. Then the king approached slowly. He was holding a sword down at his right side. He reached down and grabbed my leg to pull me toward him so he could get a better angle at my heart, but then he just stopped.

He looked at me, confused. I suddenly remembered my necklace in my boot and realized that he must have felt it while squeezing my leg. I mustered just enough strength to break away from the two men holding me down and lunged toward my boot, trying to guard him from exposing my secret.

"Hold her down!" the king ordered, and the men pinned my arms back to the ground. "She obviously has something very important that she doesn't want me to see."

I began to kick wildly and the king called more men to come and hold down my legs. He flipped up the leather on my boot to expose the little pocket that had been a secret for so long. I cried and screamed as he pulled out the necklace and then I went limp with exhaustion when I realized that it was all over.

The king held the necklace up by the chain and examined it. I heard him gasp in surprise. The men around him stared at it, intensely. The one that was holding onto my left leg let go of it in shock. I realized that it was something very important to all of them to warrant that kind of reaction.

The king stuffed the necklace back into my boot and folded down the leather quietly. He stood up and paced around for a moment or two and dropped his sword to the ground. Then he ordered his men to tie me up and put me on a horse.

I didn't understand why I was not going to be executed all of a sudden, although I realized that the reason weighed heavily on the fact that I possessed the necklace. I began to get nervous as to what this meant for me when he brought me to where he was taking me. I quickly realized that he was taking me back to his castle, but something told me that I wouldn't be making him breakfast ever again.

He returned me to my room and locked me in as soon as we got to the castle. It was only a few moments before he appeared again with the Hawk.

"Show it to me," she ordered, forcefully. I hesitated. She repeated the request again and the king took a threatening step forward to show that he was willing to take it from me by force and that it would not be a good situation for me. I leaned forward quickly and pulled the necklace out from my boot.

The Hawk immediately covered her mouth. She stared at the lion for a moment, and then put her palm out to feel its weight. She let it go shortly after and turned to the king.

"You will have to marry her," she declared, "if you want to keep your crown."

"No!" I exclaimed, panicking. They left the room, without acknowledging me, and I felt more apprehensive than I had ever been in my entire life.

CHAPTER 10

MARRIED TO THE ENEMY

They kept me locked in my room, but to make extra sure that I wouldn't be escaping any time soon they placed a guard outside my door. It wasn't the drunk this time. I never saw that man around again. I still wondered what had happened to him.

My new guard was fully serious about his job. It didn't take me long to realize that he had more at stake than just a simple punishment from the king. In fact, he seemed to genuinely care about what happened to the king. Sometimes at night I would hear the Hawk come to visit him. I could tell that they thought I was sleeping because the conversations that they had centered on things I'm sure they would have never wanted me to know, like the fact that they had been lovers for many years.

I realized during their middle of the night rendezvous that they both thought that there was a possibility that the king might be his son. While they were whispering one night I had pressed my ear to the door to hear what they were saying and that is what had come out. If that was true, even though it could never been proven, that would mean that he had no right to rule the kingdom. So where did I fit in all of this?

Every day the Hawk came to my room and asked me if I had enough punishment. When I told her I would never give in and marry the king, she would think of some new torture for me to undergo that day. My guard would carry it out. She made very sure I had no contact with anybody but the king, the guard, and her.

The king rarely did come to visit me, but when he did it was usually to let me know that he was going out to search for Rossannah and Cub. I knew that he thought that this would bother me, but I was confident that they would be able to keep themselves hidden from him.

One night, the Hawk came to get me. She told me to follow her, and I did, thinking that since I was free of my room I might be able to escape. She had thought of that already and the guard was told to walk with us as well. I was led to a room where the king and another man were waiting for me. The man, whom I had never seen before, held a large scroll in his arms. He rolled it out on a desk and I was told to sit down before it.

"Sign it," the king told me. I refused to sign it without reading it. I began to skim the words and realized at once that it was a marriage contract. I let out a loud and boisterous laugh.

"I'm not signing this," I guffawed. "Do you think I am crazy, or stupid?"

"I know you are not either," the king agreed, "which is why you are going to sign it. I have your mother."

"Where is she?" I said, skeptically. "I doubt very much that you have any ability to capture my mother."

The king waved his hand and the doors burst open. Two men carrying a gagged and helpless looking woman rushed into the room. My mother looked at me and her eyes went wide with concern and she began to thrash around widely, trying to yell something through the slip of cloth tied tightly around her mouth.

All I could hear were muffled and nervous screams.

"Sheena," I whispered, all of the hope I had managed to cling to was now gone. I picked up the pen and hastily signed the contract. It was immediately pulled out of my grasp as I finished and brought over to the king, who also signed it.

"Give me your necklace," the king ordered. I dug down into my boot pocket and produced it for him. He grabbed the chain and smugly walked over to Sheena holding it in front of her face. Her eyes went wide once again and she looked at me. Tears began to form in her eyes. Something didn't make sense.

The king brought my necklace back over to me and thrust it into my hand. He told me to put it around my neck and wear it from now on.

"Untie the mother," the king ordered. "We'll leave them alone. They will have a lot to talk about. We have what we need from her now. Even if they leave right now it won't be a big deal. It would probably be best for everybody, except for the tribes in the forest." He looked at me menacingly. He said this last part just for me, to make sure that I would stick around.

They left Sheena and me in the room by ourselves and I went over and untied her. She took the gag out and looked up at me with sorrow and anger in her eyes.

"What have you done?" she whispered, as if she would have never believed it to be true. "I was hoping that you would be the savior of us all."

"Sheena?" I asked, confused. "What are you talking about?"

"I am not Sheena!" she screamed. "I am Shyla, her twin sister." Then she softened as she reached out and held the little lion pendant hanging around my neck. "And I am also your real mother."

Memories started to flood back to me. Grandmother telling me to keep my lion pendant a secret. The first king looking at Sheena as if he recognized her. Sheena never talking about her sister. Everything started to slowly make sense, but there was still one thing I didn't understand.

"What is so important about me?" I asked Shyla, perplexed.

"There is a witness who claims that the king is not really of royal blood. She was the midwife who delivered him and says that she knew of an affair that went on between the king's wife and a stables servant at the time, although now he is one of the most loyal guards that the king has. There was a chance that the king had another heir out there somewhere, a girl who carried his mark. A lion necklace that was given to her by her mother on the day she sent her to live in the woods for safety reasons."

"I am a queen?" I whispered, confused.

"You are a queen," Shyla conceded. "And now you can rule because you have the proof of being royalty. But now that you are married, it gets a little more complicated."

"How?" I asked.

"Now you have to rule side by side with your spouse, according to our laws. If you have disagreements, it is usually put to a vote by the people of the kingdom. Decisions depend on who can gather the most loyalty from their subjects. If one of you is absent, the other makes all the major decisions."

"So what stops him from just killing me and taking over the crown?" I asked, apprehensively.

"He can't kill you if he wishes to remain in power. You have proof of being the king's true heir, but he has none. He once had a sword that belonged to the king, or at least he says he did. If he could produce the sword to show that the king had meant for him to take his place, then his power would not be in question. He needs you to hold on to his power; otherwise, the kingdom would be turned over to the next in line. If you were to die without having any children, the king's cousin would be given the crown."

I sat back and took this information in. Shyla did not say a word to me, somehow knowing that I needed this time to myself to plan what I was going to do next. When I had wrapped my mind around everything that she had told me, I looked up to her. She had stood up and was now pacing back and forth around the room. She was wrestling with something else in her mind. She looked at me and noticed that I was now watching her. She put on her best fake smile and motioned for me to stand up and follow her out of the room.

"You will have to lead me around," Shyla announced when we made it to the end of the hallway and were met with three different paths. "I've been imprisoned in a room for the last eighteen years, and before that I never stepped inside this castle before. Your father always came to me. You probably know this place better than I do."

The words *your father* sounded strange to me. It was stranger still to think about the fact that I had even seen him once, but he felt like a threat. I remembered that he had said something about a mother looking for her daughter.

"Did you send him to find me?" I asked, curious.

"I would never have done that," Shyla answered. "It was too dangerous for you here. He did go off one day searching for you, after he had heard me talking about you during a fever."

"I met him," I mentioned, off-handedly. "He was pretty adamant that you needed me. Are you sure you never wanted me to come back?"

"You would have been killed or imprisoned," Shyla roared impatiently. "No, I never wanted you back. Do not bring it up anymore. There are some things that you just don't need to know."

"I...I just want to know why you abandoned me," I whispered. Shyla stopped for a moment and looked down at her feet. She took a deep breath and then continued walking.

"If that woman wouldn't have been there to take care of you," she sighed, "I wouldn't have left you in the woods. I'm glad that she was there. That is all that you need to know. I didn't abandon you. I made sure you were taken care of."

"Are you hungry?" I said, finally giving up on the conversation. "I know where to get our food."

Even as I asked the question, I saw the king come toward us from another hallway. He reached out and grabbed my arm, and pulled me with him in the direction that he was going.

"I will need you to show your necklace to some people," he ordered. "Then you can go on and do whatever you want again."

He brought me to another room, closely followed by Shyla. A large group of people had gathered there. Most of them were old men, but the Hawk, my guard, and some woman I didn't recognize were there. The king pulled me over to the group and reached out toward my neck. I winced out of reflex, but he gently grasped the necklace and led me from person to person, showing it off to each one. He lingered at the last person in line, the woman that I didn't know.

"She signed the marriage contract this morning," the king announced as he let go of me and the necklace and then produced the contract from his vest pocket. "This is it."

I had an intense urge to grab the paper out of his hand and rip it up, but I decided that this would probably be a bad idea, especially with so many witnesses.

"This is impossible!" the woman that I didn't know shouted out. "How do we know that this girl is not an imposter as well?"

"She has his necklace," one of the old men said, "even if she is an imposter, she has one of the possessions that marks her as an heir. The king wrote it down that he would give a sword and a pendant out to his choice for heirs. That was at the time that he didn't have any children and there was the fear that he wouldn't have any children. He didn't want his kingdom to go to his nephew because he knew that his nephew is disturbed and would undoubtedly ruin it. So he had a special sword made. That sword would go to the next ruler, but just to be safe he also had the pendant around that girl's neck made in case his first choice wasn't able to rule for some reason. We were all there to watch the crafting of these items, so that we all would be able to recognize every aspect of them when they appeared again. They each have small imperfections that most people wouldn't notice, but we know them all."

"Now that my new wife has been established as the legitimate ruler," the king ordered to the woman I didn't recognize, "I want you to leave this kingdom and never come back. If you do, I will have you killed."

The woman looked around the room, looking for someone to back her up. Nobody seemed to want to help her. Then she looked at me. Her eyes were pleading with me to say something, and at that moment I realized that I did have a little power. I looked away from her. For some reason, I felt that the king's revulsion towards her held some sort of significance that if ignored would come back to haunt me if I spoke up in her defense. She realized at that moment that I wasn't going to help her and left the room in an angry rush.

After the strange woman left, the rest of the group cleared out. Shyla, the king, the Hawk, and I were the only people left in the room. There was a long silence. I didn't dare make a move to leave, and Shyla refused to leave my side. Finally, the Hawk let out a deep sigh of relief and went off to do whatever she did during the day.

"Thank you," the king turned to me. "You could have turned against me with that woman, but you didn't. You would have been the clear voice of this kingdom with those men, but you stayed on my side. I really didn't expect that. I expected this to be a fight all the way."

"I…I sensed there was something with that woman that could ruin all of our lives," I said, taken aback by his gratuity. "I was looking out for myself, not for you."

The king shrugged his shoulders and then left Shyla and me alone in the room. We both stood there for a moment and pondered about what had just happened. It was a little scary to think that now the king thought that we were allies. I wondered what he would do if he knew that in my head I was still plotting how I would save myself from his grasp.

"Let's go eat," I said to Shyla and we made our way down to the dining area.

I was expecting the same treatment that I had received from my previous captivity from the servants, but this time it was different. Before they had served me as they were told to do, but they always looked at me with repugnance and made a point to show me in little ways that they abhorred me. This time it was different. They served Shyla and me with wide smiles and seemed to look at me with admiration this time.

"What has changed?" I whispered to Shyla in my confusion.

"Everybody loves royalty here," Shyla whispered back to me in disgust. "I never really did understand it myself. I thought that it was senseless to admire somebody that didn't earn it."

"But…" I began, perplexed, "you had an affair with the king! You had me."

"Well," Shyla answered, embarrassed, "that was stupid, too. Not you, but him. I didn't know at the time how utterly disgusting he could be."

"I want to know more about it." I leaned closer to her, my attention fixed on the little she had spoken about her relationship with my father.

"You don't want to know about it," Shyla said, shortly. She scraped her fork angrily across her plate and I decided not to push the issue any farther.

After we had eaten, we wandered through the halls of the castle, wondering what to do. Neither of us had had this much freedom to do as we wished in the castle before. There really wasn't anything to do. If I had been in the forest, I would be hunting, or maybe picking berries. Cub and I would be climbing trees, or maybe I would be sitting around somewhere with Rossannah talking. Now all I had were endless empty hallways and the uncomfortable company of a mother that I had never known and who refused to tell me anything about her or my past.

I studied Shyla. She was a lot like Sheena in many ways. First of all, there were her looks. That was an obvious similarity. Her appearance was almost exactly like Sheena's, except for some minor differences. Her hands, for instance, were softer than Sheena's. Sheena had spent most of her life working with her hands, making weapons, shelters, and fires. I gathered from Shyla's hands that she had never done anything like that in her life. She must have lived an easy life. I imagined she must have been bored during a lot of it. Another difference was that Sheena had a scar on her chin. It was something that you could barely notice, but I couldn't believe that I didn't realize it wasn't there when I was being forced to sign the marriage contract.

Shyla was very quiet. That was something that she also had in common with Sheena. The difference in their absence of sound, however, held a disturbing disquietude for me. Even though Sheena was quiet unless she was barking orders or explaining something, or sometimes even letting me know that she loved me, Sheena held a happy quiet. It was the quiet that comes with busy old men whittling away at a piece of wood to make a beautiful work of art, or a child sitting down to munch on sweet fruits after a long absence from them. Shyla's quiet was something else. It was an uneasy quiet. It was a fearful quiet. It was a quiet that I wanted to break apart.

We spent that day wandering up and down the halls in total silence. When it began to get dark, and we were both tired, we found our rooms. We realized that we had only been two doors away from each other the entire time. Of course, we had never passed each other before because she had always been locked in hers, whereas I had come and gone for meals, lessons, and chores. I got a good glimpse of her room and noticed that it had many beautiful things inside of it. It looked as if she had been pampered during her imprisonment. She even had her own bathroom, but I suppose that would have been necessary if she was kept locked up for years. I looked around her room in awe.

"I know what you are thinking," she said as she noticed me gazing around the room in wonder. "I have had no shortage of luxuries in my life, but that doesn't mean anything without freedom. I never got married or had any more kids. I wasn't allowed to live my life. Remember that when *your husband* is nice to you."

I looked at her in pity as her words began to sink in. She had everything she could have ever wanted in materialistic terms, but things like clothing and trinkets don't mean anything if you are not free to love who you want. I learned that early on living in the forest. Now it seemed that I may be on the same path that she had become stuck in, except that she had made her choice to be there. I refused to believe that my life would end up the same as hers. I was going to find a way to get out of the situation.

That night I didn't sleep. I lay awake trying to think of a way to get myself and Shyla out. It was like I had gone around in a big circle, except this time it was Shyla and not Cub that I was concerned about. I didn't really know Shyla, and didn't really care for her much either. She was my mother, however, and I reasoned that had to count for something. Maybe Shyla and I would never really have a relationship at all, but I would never know that for sure unless we had a more stable environment to create one in.

I was still awake when the sun came up and light started to shine into my bedroom. I heard a soft knock on my door and called out to see who it was.

"It's me," I heard a familiar voice reply and frowned in confusion. It was the king. I wondered why he didn't just barge in like he usually did.

"Come in," I replied to the door and sat up in bed. He opened the door slowly and walked in, looking a little shy and humble.

"What's going on?" I asked, puzzled. I don't think he realized that I was asking about the change in his behavior. If he did, he didn't show that he understood.

"We have a meeting today after breakfast," he answered. "You should probably get up and eat so that we aren't late."

"A meeting?" I was now more confused than ever. "What kind of a meeting? I thought I did everything I was supposed to do."

"A war council," he answered shortly, and I saw that he was getting a little irritated with me. "Now that you are here, you have to be involved with all decision making processes. It's kind of the law."

"I really don't understand why it makes any difference that I am here." Then I remembered that I was the true heir. I told the king that I would be down to eat and so he left me alone. I got dressed and then went to Shyla's room and we walked down to the dining area in silence.

We sat at the table and ate in quiet, Shyla, the king, the Hawk, and me. Every bite was excruciatingly soundless, or maybe it seemed that way because of the pounding in my brain. The changes in the room came at me from every angle and beat themselves into my mind, and if it weren't for that unbearable silence I may have been able to cope with it. There sat Shyla, my mother, but not my mother. BANG. She looked like my mother, but she isn't Sheena. BAM. There was the Hawk, sitting across from me, her authoritative demeanor was now gone. POW. Then there were the servants, smiling and ecstatic to assist me with whatever I wanted. SMACK. Worst of all, there sat the king on the corner, watching me, a mixture of curiosity, respect, and irritation painting his face in waves. Maybe there was a little jealousy somewhere in there as well. This was the deathblow.

"I think I'm going to be sick," I stammered and rushed off to find the nearest bathroom. I heard the footsteps of four or five of the servants following close behind me. As I leaned over the toilet in preparation for the reappearance of everything that I had just eaten, I heard them chattering with concern behind me. Then I felt cool, dry hands on my neck reaching to pull my hair back. When I finished, I turned around to see who had helped me and came face to face with the servant who had seemed to hate me the most during my previous stay, a tiny, white-haired old woman named Ashlee.

"Would you like me to put your hair up for you," Ashlee asked, hopefully, "in case you get sick again?"

"No, I'm fine now," I said, quickly, waving her away. "I just didn't get any sleep last night."

Her face fell and I felt slightly ashamed of myself for being so abruptly defensive against this woman who was only a sad product of the society she grew up in. I realized that many of the people that lived here were only sheep in need of extreme guidance. They needed a shepherd to tell them how to think, to dress, to talk, and even to feel. Her love for me was like that of a misguided dog, looking at his master for praise. Instead of praising her, I scolded her. I let her down.

"Are you ready?" The king appeared in the doorway of the bathroom. Instantly, the faces of the servants were distorted into looks of confusion as they darted from the king to me. I tried to hide my amusement as I thought of the servants as puppies who couldn't choose between masters. Maybe if I had a scrap of food in my pocket I could get them to all turn on him.

"I guess," I answered. I held out my hand to Ashlee and let her help me up. It was the best thing I could think to do to make up for my refusal of her last attempt at affection. She seemed thrilled at my bid for her assistance.

We went back to the same room where the king had presented me to the room full of old men. Now it was filled with people of all genders, ages, and sizes. A long table had been placed at one end of the room, and the rest of the space had been filled with rows of chairs facing the table. The old men that had authenticated my right to rule were all sitting there facing the rows of people sitting in the chairs, and two seats in the middle of the table were left open.

The king led me toward the table and we sat down in the two empty chairs. The previously noisy room then erupted into silence. It was instantaneous as we sat down. It was as if one giant hand had reached out and cupped the mouths of every single person in the room. There was no straggling conversation to hush, not even a break away whisper. No one coughed or sneezed and no sound of shuffling feet found its way to my ears. There was not one sound that anybody could expect from a group of people this large. The collective silence unnerved me and I looked at the crowd, desperate for any sound. I began to fear that the pounding from breakfast would come back.

"We will begin," the king began, commandingly.

"Excuse me," the old man sitting beside me spoke up, clearing his throat, "but is it really your place to start the meetings anymore."

Every eye turned towards me. Waiting. Expecting. I had no clue what I was supposed to do. I had no clue why I was here. I wasn't their leader. I didn't want to be their leader. I just wanted to go home.

"I will turn this meeting over to…my husband," I managed to stammer out. They all turned their attention back towards him. I sighed in relief.

"We are here to discuss the punishment of a war criminal," the king boomed. "As she was once a part of our own population, I recommend that the punishment be execution to discourage others from following her example." There was the sound of agreement throughout the room. Then all eyes trained on me again for what I assume was my consent.

"I…I don't know," I admitted.

"Bring her in," the old man beside me ordered. "Maybe if the Queen sees her she will be able to make a more informed decision on her stance of the situation." I looked at the man beside me and he winked at me, knowingly.

Then the guards brought her in, bloody and beaten, but I would know her anywhere. Rossannah.

"No execution!" I roared, not entirely sure of what I was doing. I looked over at the old man beside me and he exchanged a look of understanding with me.

"State the case for this girl's life," he ordered me.

"What she did was to save my life so that I could be discovered," I answered, instantly.

"There is dissention in the voices of our two rulers, her life will be put to a vote," the old man announced. "All opposed to spare this girl's life on the grounds that she kept the heir to the throne in one piece raise your hand." Every person in the room except for the king raised their hands. The old man next

to me looked satisfied. Rossannah was safe,
but I knew that whatever peace that I had
previously created with the king was now
destroyed.

CHAPTER 11

SAVING ROSSANNAH SAVING ME

Rossannah was in my bed. Her face was swollen and bloody and that wasn't even the worst of it. She had bruises from head to toe and there were deep cuts in her back where the whips had touched it. She smelled of feces and urine because she had been tied up and not allowed to use the bathroom.

Shyla and I removed her clothing and I instructed my new shadow, Ashlee, to burn it and bring her new clothes. Shyla and I then wrapped her in my blankets and helped her to the bathroom where we had run a bathtub full of hot water. As we tried to lower her down into the tub, she began to scream and arched away from it as the hot water touched her sore and open wounds. We helped her out again and Shyla helped her sit up as I dipped a wash cloth into the tub and washed around her wounds, scrubbing away the repugnancy as best I could without having to submerge her.

"I can't get rid of the smell," I complained to Shyla.

"We will have to put her in the shower," she sighed.

"But she can't stand it," I argued.

"Cold water," Shyla said. "It will still hurt, but she needs to get clean to prevent infection. It will feel better than the hot water. Hopefully she will pass out and we can use soap."

We ran the shower and forced Rossannah, half-unconscious but still fighting into it.

Shyla had a strength that I hadn't expected in her and she held Rossannah's wriggling body as I applied the stinging soap to it. It took a while to do because of all of the struggling but we eventually finished and then went about the equally trying task of drying her off. It was as if every inch of Rossannah's body was bursting with pain and she couldn't stand to be touched.

Ashlee appeared with the new clothes that I had ordered her to get. I made a move to put them on Rossannah but Shyla stopped me.

"No," Shyla ordered, "let's let her be naked for a while. We'll need new blankets and sheets for her to lie on though. We should probably get a healer to check out her wounds. Maybe they can do something to make the pain less."

I agreed with Shyla and sent Ashlee out to get the things that Shyla had mentioned. We wrapped Rossannah in towels and brought her back to my room, and held her while we waited for servants to strip my bed and put fresh linens on it. Then we put Rossannah in my bed on her stomach so we wouldn't upset the whip marks on her back. She closed her eyes and went to sleep.

The healer came and put something on her back and checked her over. He mentioned that she was lucky she didn't have any broken bones. Then he made her swallow something and she seemed to be in less pain. He gave me a bottle and told me when to give her the little pills inside. He promised to come back and check on her every day.

At night, I slept on the floor beside her so that I wouldn't accidently touch her wounds and cause her pain. In the morning, Shyla would come and sit with her when I couldn't be with her. I made sure that someone was with Rossannah at all times because in her fragile state she could easily become a victim of the king or his mother and people would just believe that she had died. I couldn't let that happen.

The king would show up every now and then to "check" on Rossannah's progress, but I knew that he was just trying to catch her at a time when she had no defense. Even though he didn't outwardly show his disdain for me, I could tell that he wanted nothing more than to hurt me. Killing Rossannah would be an opportunity to do that.

Eventually, Rossannah began to get better. She started to talk a little, here and there. Sometimes she would request water or food. I was ecstatic the night that she rolled over onto her back in her sleep and didn't even wake up in pain. She still felt weak though.

"Are Cub and Sheena alright?" I asked her when I felt she was strong enough to talk about what had happened.

"What? Oh…yeah, they're fine," She answered. "It was me. I was the only one caught. They tried to stop me."

"What happened?" I asked.

"Some of the people in the tribe got scared," she replied, "before we were supposed to rescue you. They turned on the rest of us. They kept us from going. They said if he had you he would probably leave the rest of us alone. We tried to get to you…but there were too many people who agreed with them. When it was all over, it was too late. Sheena and Cub said that you were probably dead by then. I didn't think that you were. I wanted to go after you. Sheena said if you weren't dead that you would be able to take care of yourself because you were smart. They told me to stay. I couldn't stay, so I waited until everybody was asleep. I used everything you had taught me about the forest and I found my way back here. As soon as they saw me, they arrested me. They beat me and tried to get me to tell them where the tribe was that had been hiding us. I was going to come and rescue you. Maybe I was foolish. You're the Queen now?"

Her speech was broken and confused. Every sentence was broken with a pause as she searched for the words to begin the next one. I looked at her face which had now been healed without a slight trace that any damage had been done except for her eyes. Her emerald eyes were now dulled by the hint of the emotional scars left behind. I had come from the forest. I had known this life for as long as I remember. I had to hide from the world for years, from the time of my birth. This was her first taste of the pure hatred that others felt for her. She had come back, expecting that nothing too bad would happen to her, and this is what she had found. I could see that she felt betrayed. She was supposed to be one of them, but you can't have your two feet in separate worlds without expecting to be ripped apart.

I leaned over to kiss her, as I would often do when Cub was distraught. My lips touched her forehead and lingered there as I swallowed back my regrets that she would have to learn about war this way. People like her shouldn't have to be caught in the middle of it. People like her should be able to watch from the sidelines with no real understanding as to what the fighting really means. I was built for this, as were the others who were raised in the forest. Then it dawned on me. That is why the king hated us so much. We were the only people who possessed the ability to stand up to him.

I don't know how long I stood there like that, with my lips pressed firmly against Rossannah's forehead, contemplating my new understanding of the inner workings of the king before I felt the tender, newly weathered hands reach quietly for my face and rest on my check. I looked at Rossannah's face and lost my own hands in her beautiful strawberry blonde hair and then we kissed. It was a real kiss, soft and intimate, the way a man and a woman are supposed to kiss. It was tender and beautiful and unrehearsed, unlike the many kisses that I had shared with Joseph, but best of all, it was true. It was like I had been living in a world full of clouds, never knowing the sun, but at this moment the sky opened up and I could feel golden rays all over my body. That is what that kiss was like.

When it was over, it felt as if the clouds swallowed me back up again. We pulled away from each other, confusion pulsing unconcealed on both of our faces. For the first time since we had met, we were both too shy to speak to each other. I wondered which one of us would be the one to break the silence. Which one of us would find the courage to explore what had just happened to us?

"I don't know why I did that," Rossannah spoke up. Her normal speech had returned to her. It was as if that kiss had thrust her back into a place where what had happened to her physical body was just a minimal irritation on her emotional stability.

"I don't know why I let you," I conceded. Then we both just began to laugh. We shrugged off that moment as a one-time occurrence and began to talk, as if we were us. But we weren't us, not anymore. Now we were other people entirely, other people that tried to ignore the very thing that defined who we had become. We attempted to be us, but those other people shined through more and more every day as Rossannah became stronger and I became more overwhelmed with responsibility that I didn't want and the one-time occurrences happened more often behind closed doors. Eventually we just gave up and let those other people have their ways. Then we just accepted them as the new us. Then we decided to love them. It wasn't a fast transition, but it was one that I had been dying for my entire life.

When Rossannah was fully healed, the king insisted that she go back to live with her father, who had once again returned. I couldn't handle the thought of losing her so I argued with him about it. I had learned over the past few weeks that I had just as many if not more rights as he did and I started to slowly assert them. This seemed to annoy him immensely but he couldn't do or say anything to force me to change the force with which I began to embrace my new found sense of power.

"She should at least be staying in her own room," he argued with me. "She's well now, and she can take care of herself. If you have to have her around at least give her a room next to yours or something. People don't really expect the queen to have a roommate. There is an etiquette here. You are going to be expected to act a certain way. You're not really supposed to have friends. If you had been groomed for your position you would have known that."

He enunciated his last sentence with vigor, throwing his hands up in the air. It was true. He had been the one who had been taught from birth to be a leader. I was thrust into this as a last ditch effort for him to hold onto his power. I couldn't feel sorry for him though. What he chose to do with the power that he had been handed was nothing short of barbaric. Still, I gave some thought as to what he had been trying to communicate to me and decided that even though I could never fully trust him or his motives, I had to admit to myself that for the sake of living a semi-peaceful existence in a world I couldn't fully control that I had to make some compromises with it to maintain it.

That night I broke the news to Rossannah that she would be moving into the room that was between Shyla's room and my own. It was a strategic move that not only kept us in close proximity to each other and would allow us to sneak in and out of each other's rooms without being detected, but also added extra protection because Shyla was on the other side. Even though I was learning that the king was mostly smoke and no fire, I still felt safer knowing that if Rossannah ever screamed, we would both be able to be there to rescue her.

Rossannah wasn't thrilled with the idea. She argued that I was letting him set all of the rules. I think that even though she argued that point she knew that it wasn't true. If he had his way she wouldn't even be close, and I would let go of everybody that I

had ever known and do things his way all of
the time.

   The truth was that it was good for us to
be in separate rooms because I had a whole
mess of people watching me now and I was
supposed to be married to the king. I didn't
know how my "subjects" would react to my
strange infidelities. Now I was winning most
of the battles when it came to making
decisions. The people really took to me on
the grounds that I was the "real" ruler. I
had been able to completely stop the king from
hunting down the tribes in the forests. It
was nice to have control. The king would
argue his point and I would argue mine and we
would leave it up to the population to decide.
I fully realized that my affair with Rossannah
could possibly sway all votes in his
direction.

   The first night of our separation was
agonizing. I had gotten used to Rossannah
being beside me all night. Now we had to
content ourselves with a couple of hours
before letting go to be by ourselves in our
own beds. I suppose we could have easily
allowed ourselves one or two nights of
sleepovers but the risk seemed too great.
While Rossannah was sick we didn't ever think
about these things, but the king's constant
reminders of how I should be acting now that
Rossannah was well kept us from doing things
that we would be hard-pressed to view as
mistakes if we were ever caught.

CHAPTER 12

CAUGHT...FINALLY

Years went by. I never imagined that
years could seem so short and so long at the
same time. Now here I was on my twenty-fifth
birthday contemplating how the days could seem
so long and the nights could seem so short
even when the winter months mercifully greatly
expanded the darkness.

I spent a lot of time looking back on the
last few years that day. There had been so
many good things that I had accomplished, and
every little bit of it I had to do with a
fight. There were small battles that I just
couldn't win because people get stuck in their
ways and some things just can never be
changed, but for the most part my forest and
my people were safe. The people jumped at my
suggestion that there should be no war against
them anymore, but there were still minor
restrictions against them, which I thought
were silly because it really didn't affect
them at all.

I remembered the day four years before
that Sheena and Cub had come to visit me for
the first time without fear of being
imprisoned or hurt. They walked right up to
the castle and requested to meet with me. We
were eating lunch when they were led into the
dining room and I gasped at the sight of them.
Rossannah and I both jumped up and the four of
us hugged and held each other while Shyla, the
Hawk, and the king watched with stupid looks
on their faces.

As we let go of each other I saw Shyla rise from the table from the corner of my eye. She had a look on her face as if she had seen a ghost as she slowly approached us.

"Who is this woman with my face?" Sheena breathed as she noticed Shyla for the first time. I felt a little guilty when I realized that the last time I had seen Sheena when Cub, Rossannah, and I had escaped, I had forgotten about the one conversation that I had with Shyla when she had informed me that she was Sheena's twin sister. I bit my lip in shame and backed away from them as Shyla glided to a stop in front of Sheena. Sheena's face contorted in confusion as Shyla gingerly grasped both of Sheena's hands and turned them to lie palms up in her own hands. Then Shyla brought Sheena's hands up to her mouth and planted a soft kiss on her open palms, lingering a while in each one. Sheena's face erupted into instant recognition and her eyes began to fill with tears.

"Oh Shy!" Sheena exclaimed. "I was sure you were dead." She brought Shyla's palms to her own mouth, reciprocating the gesture that Shyla had just completed.

It was a confusing custom, but one that I saw them practice countless times after that day. That is how they greeted each other whenever they had been away from each other a long time. I had never seen anybody do this before so I surmised that it was something that was unique to them.

That night Shyla and I explained to Sheena that she was my biological mother and they laughed about how ironic it was that I should end up in Sheena's arms. I had recently started to see Shyla as a long lost aunt, even though in truth it was Sheena who was my aunt. Sheena had raised me and would always be my mother.

Cub and Sheena went back to the forest after a brief stay. They begged Shyla, Rossannah, and me to go with them. I told them I couldn't leave the fate of our tribes in the hands of the king. I told Shyla and Rossannah that they were free to leave if they wanted, but Shyla had been raised here and couldn't see any other way to live and Rossannah wouldn't leave me. I was relieved that Rossannah was so loyal, but sometimes I regretted that Shyla was around.

Cub and Sheena came back many times after that, and always stayed for a day or two. Sometimes Sheena would come by herself, and sometimes Cub would come alone. Cub seemed to come around more as she began to get older and more independent. She was gaining the forest strength and I realized that I was beginning to feel a little jealous of her and the fact that she would get to live out her life in freedom. Her only obligations were that of the tribe. I missed those obligations.

Cub visited a few weeks before I had turned twenty-five. This time she had come with a boy. She had called him her boyfriend. I regretted not being around to see this milestone take place.

Now I was twenty-five, the age at which most women in my tribe started to think about having a child. I was just contemplating the last few years. It wasn't as if I didn't think about that kind of thing, but thinking about it and accomplishing it presented a problem. I had just decided that I wouldn't think about it anymore because it wasn't likely to happen.

I wasn't the only one thinking about it, though. As I was sitting in the dining area eating my lunch with Rossannah, the king approached me cautiously.

"We should probably think about an heir," he blurted out as he sat down across from us and motioned to the servants that he wished to be served. I set my fork down on the plate nonchalantly and thought for a moment.

"What about that cousin that everybody is always talking about?" I answered. "If something were to happen to me he could take over."

"No," he responded, irritated. "That's not what I meant. I meant a real heir. Blood." It took a while for what he was saying to sink in.

"I don't think so," I spat out. "No way." Rossannah was sitting beside me quietly. I looked over in her direction and we exchanged looks of horror.

"It's just my cousin…I mean *your cousin* Hector isn't really an ideal candidate to take over. It would be better to have someone that we could teach from birth." He was pleading with me now. He didn't seem to understand that I wouldn't give in. To him, this was part of our job as rulers. I, however, had never wanted this job, but since I got to make many of the rules there were aspects of this job that I felt I could just ignore as long as it didn't interfere with my protection of my people.

"We will find someone then," I maintained. "I'm not going to have a child with you. If this necklace can identify me as the next ruler it can do the same for somebody else."

"The training has to be constant. We can't let outside forces interfere with what we are trying to do. It would be easier if it were our own child. People aren't just going to hand their children over to us," he argued.

"We'll see," I said, dismissing him.

"I'll invite Hector to the castle," the king replied, angrily, "maybe you will change your mind then." Then he stormed off to go and write his letter inviting the cousin to come and stay with us for a few weeks.

"I doubt it," I called after him. When he was out of earshot Rossannah and I erupted into a fit of giggles.

"What is he, crazy?" Rossannah laughed. She lifted her water glass to her lips and took a drink but had to spit the water out again because she couldn't control her laughter.

"He's acting as if we have a real marriage or something," I worried, sobering up. "I don't know, Rossannah, this could be trouble. I don't know if it is possible but he may try to take this issue to council. I don't know how people would react to it." Rossannah stopped laughing, which troubled me even more than I already was. I had hoped that she would find my apprehension ridiculous and break out into a new fit of guffaws, but she only contributed to my fear that I did have something to be anxious about.

"Maybe this is just a plot," Rossannah presented, "to prove that he is the only one that really cares about the kingdom. If he gets the people back on his side he could probably do just about whatever he wanted. If he takes it to council, maybe you should just agree to it. He might back off. Even if you do agree to it in public, it doesn't mean that

you have to go through with it. It would be
his word against yours, and the people like
you better."

"I wish Sheena was here," I fretted, "I
need her to tell me what to do."

"Maybe I could help," Shyla offered as
she walked into the dining area and sat down.
"What is the problem?"

"It's nothing," I said defensively and we
all ate the rest of the meal in silence. I
had gotten used to shutting Shyla out of my
life. At times she could be helpful and warm,
but she was mostly cold and distant. I had
hoped that we would have been able to ignite
some sort of friendship between us, but it was
if she was always trying to make a decision
about whether or not she wanted me in her
life. I had given up and come to the
conclusion that I didn't want to deal with her
instability. I did make an effort whenever
Sheena was around to act as if there was
nothing wrong with my relationship with Shyla
to put Sheena's mind at ease. Sheena only saw
the warm part of Shyla.

After lunch, Rossannah and I decided to
take a walk out in the fields where all of the
crops were grown. We did this every day. We
walked along the edge of the forests and
sighed at our longing to be in them.

Then I had to get back to work. I sat in
the big room behind the table next to the king
while people approached us one by one and
rattled off their silly little problems. We
wrote them down one by one and promised to
come up with a decision by the next council.
We sorted out everything from disputes over
property to stupid little husband and wife
arguments over how to discipline children. I
couldn't care less about these issues. In the

forest we sorted these things out for ourselves. For the most part, I allowed the king to take care of everything. He stood up during council day and boomed in his own self-important way how things should be done. We had both realized that we didn't even need to talk about it. The only time I would ever speak up was if it had anything to do with my precious forest. I only acted as if I was listening to these pathetically dependent people to get their votes for the times that I needed them.

I was ecstatic when supper came. It had been an unbelievably cruel day filled with miniscule problems that I had to pretend to care about. I happily took my place in between Rossannah and Shyla and made my mind up to hurry through my meal so that I could scamper off to my room and spend time with Rossannah. She seemed to realize that I was in an excruciating need to get away from that table as quickly as possible and began shoveling food into her mouth at the same rate that I was.

"I sent the letter off to Hector," the king mentioned as he led the Hawk into the dining area and they both sat down.

"Mm hmm." I barely acknowledged him through my mouthful of venison, a rare treat that was now served for my enjoyment.

"He will probably be here in a week or two," he continued, ignoring my disinterest in the subject.

"Mm hmm." I said again, equally unimpressed. He scoffed at my table manners and went about eating his own supper which had just been placed in front of him.

"Happy birthday," the Hawk said, stiffly. "You are twenty-five now? Is that right,

Joby? That is a great age to have children. Actually, I would think that twenty or twenty-one would be about the *right* age to have your first child, but to each their own." I stopped eating.

"I don't really see how it is any of your business," I fumed.

"I just thought that you might want to start thinking about it," The Hawk offered innocently.

"Well, I don't," I said, irritated at her attempt at a pleasant motherly conversation. She had recently adopted this manner of speaking to me while at the same time slipping in little rude innuendos of what I should be doing.

"I'm finished," Rossannah chirped. "Excuse me." She got up and left the table. I looked down at my plate, realizing that I had been sucked into yet another argument with the Hawk and lost sight of what I was trying to do. I took two more bites of what I had left on my plate and decided that I didn't want anymore.

I got up and left the table without a word to anyone. I managed to smile at Ashlee on my way out of the dining area to show my appreciation. She beamed back at me with pride.

"Goodnight," Shyla called after me. I waved my hand to acknowledge her but didn't speak.

Rossannah was already waiting in my room when I got there. We sat down on the bed together and began to talk about our day. Rossannah had gone to see her father after lunch because he had been sick. I told her about the most pathetic problems that had come to me during that day. Then we began to kiss.

Most days our lovemaking was soft and tender, but on the days where we had both experienced a constant stream of frustration it was passionate and unpredictable. Today we both had our fair share of woes so we took them out on our bodies in a way that could only increase our pleasure.

"What are you doing?" an angry voice bellowed at us and we were shocked out of our fantasy as we turned to face the accusing figure standing in my doorway.

"What are you doing?" Shyla boomed again as she slammed the door shut behind her. "I can hear you two all the way down the hall. Do you know what would happen if somebody besides me would have walked in on you?"

Shyla walked toward the bed and then bent over to pick up Rossannah's dress at the foot of it and threw it at her.

"Put it on and go to your own room," she ordered her forcefully. Rossannah got dressed quickly and scurried away as Shyla glared at her.

"You don't seem to be happy unless you are trying to back yourself against a wall, do you?" Shyla accused furiously. "When did Rossannah and you start this?"

"A long time ago," I admitted. "Years ago."

"Well it needs to stop now," Shyla ordered.

"I…It can't," I said, fumbling with my words. I needed to make Shyla understand that Rossannah was as important to me as food, or air.

"Damn it, Joby! There are some things that you don't understand," Shyla argued. "It's just not allowed anymore."

"Anymore?"

"I'm sorry," Shyla retracted. "I misspoke…I meant to say it's just not allowed."

"You said anymore and you meant it," I pressed. "Why did you say anymore? Were there other people like us?"

"There were or are," Shyla softened, "but it's a dangerous thing to be. It used to be accepted, but something happened and now it isn't. That is all that you need to know. Just know that if you don't end it, it could cause huge problems and even being a queen can't protect you from the backlash."

"I don't care," I cried, tears welling up in my eyes.

"That is unfortunate," Shyla sighed and walked back toward my door. She stopped in the doorway and then turned her head in my direction.

"I will try to help you keep this a secret," she whispered, sadly, "if you try to be more careful." Then she walked out and shut the door behind her, giving me one last worried glance before she did.

Rossannah returned to my room after she heard the door close to Shyla's room. I told her about the conversation that we had just had and we both agreed to lay low for a while. Rossannah immediately went back to her own room and we only spent time alone together during our walks in the fields for a while.

Chapter 13

Hector

A week and a half after the night Shyla had caught us, Hector arrived and I was glad. The king had been looming over me at every turn, warning me that he was coming as if it was supposed to strike some sort of impending doom in my heart. His appearance signaled the end of the king's constant reminders which he seemed to track me down every hour to give. At last I would get some peace.

Rossannah and I were wandering around the fields, talking about the growth of the plants. It was a topic I didn't know anything about so I listened and nodded my head to act as if I understood. We looked up to see him riding a jet black horse which he rushed into the stables.

"Let's go!" I cried to Rossannah, anticipating that this was the psychopath that the king was so adamantly against taking over his precious kingdom.

We ran to the stables, hand in hand, laughing as we tripped twice on clumps of dirt or rocks that hadn't been removed. The first time Rossannah tripped and brought me down with her, and then I returned the favor as we neared the stables.

We got our first good look at him when we burst through the stable doors. It was all new. I had never stepped foot in the stables before as I had never particularly cared for horses.

Hector was handing the reins of his shiny black stallion to none other than the man who had guarded me before I signed my marriage contract with the king. I was shocked. I had thought that he was a soldier or something to that extent. It turns out he was no more than the servant who took care of the horses. I allowed myself to wonder for a moment what would possess the Hawk to have an affair with a man who worked for her when she was so adamant against speaking with the servants.

"Hello, I'm Joby," I introduced myself as he finished talking to my guard. He had very specific instructions as to how to take care of his horse.

He looked at me for a moment, considering me, and then his face erupted into a look of excitement. He charged at me like a mad bull and I instinctively took two steps back before he wrapped his arms around my waist and swung me around in a gigantic hug.

I was taken aback by everything about him. I had expected someone totally different. He had blonde hair and blue eyes and when I had imagined him I thought that he would look more like the king.

He was also very charming. We walked around the fields together with Rossannah and he spoke animatedly about what life was like where he came from. He drew us in as he talked about sports and horseback riding and parties. He seemed to live his life on a playground and was adamant to invite others to come and join him.

His speech was another thing I hadn't imagined as well. It was exciting and boastful. His sentences were sometimes cut off and forgotten if he saw something that interested him and he would go off on another subject entirely. The king's speech was always very mechanical and deliberate. I could see why the king would think that this man was disturbed. I decided that I liked this man.

"It's time for me to go to the council, I think," I said as I looked up at the sun. I invited Hector to go with me. I assumed that he might as well see what the protocol was if he was going to be the person who took over in the event of my death. He thanked me warmly and we parted with Rossannah to make our way to the big room.

We met up with the king about half way to the big room. He approached us and we stopped to chat before going to council.

"So I see you've met Hector," the king smiled, knowingly, "Doesn't he make a good first impression?"

I glared at him. I didn't know what he was insinuating, but I didn't like it. I was only allowed to contemplate it for a moment before I saw Hector lunge from beside me toward the king and thrust his fist at his face. The king winced as the fist caught him in the jaw and glared at Hector as he rubbed it to alleviate some of the pain that the blow had caused.

"Nice to see you again, Hector." the king said as if this exchange was normal. Then he started to walk off to the big room. I looked at Hector for an explanation.

"I always knew there was something up with him," Hector explained to me in an accusatory tone. "It was his eyes. Nobody in our family has those eyes. I just would like to know how he did it, and how he managed to get himself back in power."

"Let's not talk about that," I flushed. I was embarrassed by my folly with the marriage contract. Still, I liked this man who attacked the king. I had wanted to do that for as long as I could remember.

We walked into the big room where council was held and I motioned for Hector to sit down with the population. I took my normal place behind the table. As I sat the king gave me an "I told you so" look. I looked away from him trying to hide the satisfaction on my face. The king's issue with Hector was his problem, not mine. I liked Hector.

"Do you see?" the king whispered to me after council was over. "He is unstable. He is happy one moment and he goes off into rages the next."

"Maybe just with you," I countered. "You have that effect on people."

"Hmph. You'll see. He's not through yet," the king promised me.

Two weeks went by and I didn't see anything wrong with Hector. Every day the king continued to promise me that I would see what was wrong with him sooner or later. At the time I thought that it was just wishful thinking on his part, but the time finally did come when Hector began to show his true nature. From then on it was a downward spiral of one incident after another.

It all started during breakfast one morning. The king, Rossannah, Shyla, Hector, and I had been having an uneventful meal. The Hawk had taken meals in her bedroom since Hector had arrived.

It was a quick fluid movement. If not for the actions that had followed it I would have dismissed it as an accident. The king motioned Ashlee to come and serve him more oatmeal. Ashlee obliged and on her way back to her spot, Hector nonchalantly stuck out his foot as he gulped down another spoonful of oatmeal. He caught Ashlee's legs. The pot of oatmeal flew up into the air and across the room, and Ashlee, not being able to catch herself, landed face first into the hard floor. She sat up sputtering and crying as blood poured out of her nose.

"Oh Ashlee!" I called out, running to her side with my cloth napkin. "Are you alright?" I held my cloth napkin up to the nose of this poor, mousy old woman and looked up at Hector, frowning in confusion.

"Hector, did you have to?" the king scolded as he also rushed to Ashlee's side and helped me bring her to her feet.

"Oh relax, man." Hector replied, slowly sliding his foot back under the table into its proper place. "She's only a servant. It was good for a laugh."

I opened my mouth to yell at him, but the king put his arm on my shoulder as a warning to keep my feelings to myself and for the first time since we met I completely trusted him. It was an uneasy feeling that I would rarely experience but I allowed it to take over in moments where the nature of the situation called for it.

"Let's get her to a bathroom and clean her up," the king ordered. "Shyla…Rossannah…would you mind helping. I think the majority of us are finished eating, servants can go to the kitchen and start clean up there." I realized that he was trying to clear everyone out of the room so that they wouldn't be left alone with Hector. For the first time I saw that the king had a protective nature about him and wondered what it would have been like to grow up with him as an older brother, which was probably what would have happened if my mother had not left me in the woods with Grandmother.

We left Hector there in the dining area, completely oblivious to the fact that he had done anything wrong. I looked back at him in disgust as we all shuffled in a little group, each holding on to Ashlee in some comforting way as she blubbered in dismay over the sight of her own blood and the confusion over what had just happened to her. Hector just sat there, calmly eating his meal. Each spoonful was carried deliberately to his mouth without a second thought. I wondered how someone could do something so horrible and then carry on as if nothing had ever happened.

"It's starting," the king informed us when we were all in the bathroom, safely out of earshot of Hector. "Nobody is alone with Hector for at least a couple of days, understand?" We all nodded in agreement, still confused as to what was happening.

"Ashlee, after you get cleaned up, you bring out the special table." He addressed Ashlee as if they had done this before. She responded as if this was a normal part of her day, as if she was expecting this all along.

I washed Ashlee's face and she looked at me in appreciation. Great. Just another reason for her to follow me around. I guess it wasn't normal for someone in charge to take such an interest in someone so low on the totem pole, unless of course it was the kind of interest Hector took in them. The king didn't seem to want to participate in Ashlee's renovation. He simply handed it over to Ashlee and watched as I took it out of her hands to clean her so she wouldn't have to look at herself in the mirror.

By lunch I noticed the new table. It must have been made specifically for the occasion of Hector's visits. It looked like a normal table, but when you pushed your chair in after you sat down there were solid slabs of wood blocking you in from each side. It would be impossible to slide your foot out without pulling yourself out first. Hector must have a problem with tripping people.

The king told Ashlee that she didn't have to serve the meals while Hector was around. She refused the kindness. There was no way that Ashlee was going to miss out on the small interaction that she had with us. However, you could tell she was nervous because when she passed Hector her hands would shake a little and you could hear the top on the pot she was carrying shake in fear against it. It was disquieting to all of us.

Over the next three days, servants steered around Hector when he would pass them. Sometimes he would start to scoot out from his place at the table and we knew to halt any requests for seconds. We would finish eating what we had and wait for him to get up and leave the table.

His demeanor was different as well. He was sullen and prone to outbursts of screaming for no reason. Anything could set him off. I avoided him at all costs.

Then after three days, he was his old self again. The regular table came back. His charming smile came back. Everything I had liked about him came back, but my warmth towards him had changed forever.

"What is wrong with him?" I asked the king over supper one night, when he had left the table and I was sure he was far enough away so he couldn't hear me.

"Sometimes he is Hector," the king explained, "and sometimes he is not Hector."

"What is that supposed to mean?"

"Hector is sweet, charming, playful, and all-around a good person," the king clarified, "but he shares his body with Victor, Mary, Juniper, Todd, and sometimes…very rarely…Roman. I guess there are others, but those are the ones that I have seen."

"That doesn't make any sense," I countered.

"They all have their quirks and fetishes," the king went on, ignoring my comment, "and for the most part *we* are safe. They mostly act out on people that are weaker than they are…servants, slaves, and children. Stay away from Roman if you can help it, he's the reason mother doesn't eat with us when Hector comes to visit."

"So Roman was the one that came out?" I wondered.

"No, that was Victor," the king corrected me. "He likes to torture servants. Mary likes to torture slaves. Juniper likes to attack the elderly. Todd likes to hurt children."

"What about Roman?" I prodded.

"Don't worry about Roman," he assured me. "Roman never comes out."

"How do I know which one is which?" I asked.

"They each have their own batch of crazy. You'll learn to recognize them."

"What is he still doing here?" Rossannah spoke up angrily from beside me. I jumped, startled. I had forgotten that Rossannah and Shyla were still at the table with us.

"He's here to prove a point," the king said, defending his decision to have Hector in our presence. "I don't think she gets it yet."

Over the course of the next few months we were exposed to the horrors of Hector's personalities. I grew accustomed to waking up in the morning and asking Hector over breakfast what his name was. Most of the time he would laugh and say that he was Hector, because he didn't know about his other personalities, although they all knew about him. He thought it was some sort of game when I would ask him these questions. The king was impressed with this because up until I had implemented this simple, yet effective method, no one had thought of it. This gave us a good idea of what we would be dealing with that day, and who we would have to keep him away from. We even managed to capture a few new personalities and I began to write them down in a book to help us deal with the issues that they brought with them when they appeared. Even though it helped, it wasn't fool proof because he could experience changes in personality throughout the day, but he usually woke up in the morning with the personality he would carry until he went to bed at night.

Hector's presence brought out something that I had ignored until the king had mentioned it being the target of one of Hector's personalities. Slaves. I had known of their presence in all of my years living there, but never seen them. I learned later that this was because they were often hidden away in chores that were not visible to most people. I had felt as if I had been the only one forced to do labor without any pay when I was brought back after the war, but I learned later that there were entire communities in the kingdom that were created and maintained on the backs of slaves. It left me feeling sick to my stomach. I decided that this was one of the things that I needed to change with my power.

"They are not even born into it," the king argued with me when I brought it up to him. It was the first time that I ever sought him out to discuss something that had to do with his part of the world and not mine. "When somebody breaks the law, they get sentenced to slavery. It deters people from doing it and also rewards people for being good. It's a win/win situation for everybody. I don't understand your problem with it."

"I lived it," I announced. "For two years! I was forced to do whatever was expected of me! I'm still living it! You have no idea what that's like."

"I have every idea what it's like!" the king bellowed back and stormed off. He found me again two hours later and we discussed it more calmly.

"Before we started this slavery thing," he explained, "we executed anyone who broke the law. Laws are placed there for the protection of everyone. We make them slaves and give them to people who are struggling to pay people to work for them. They feed them and clothe them and save money and make money at the same time. There is a standard that the slaveholders have to meet or else they lose their slaves. We then also have someone constantly watching them to make sure that they don't get out of line again. It's humane."

"I understand the need for a punishment," I countered, "but forcing someone to work for you is never humane."

"It's better than killing them," He argued again.

"That depends on the person," I answered. "I think I would rather die than spend my life in captivity." He considered this for a moment.

"Let's go visit a slave community," he said, "I will show you it isn't as bad as you think it is. It's not like what I did with you. We have always been at war, and I had to try to rein you in some way. This is better than that."

I agreed to tour a community with him. We loaded Hector in a carriage with us so that we could monitor him and started on a two-day journey. We left Rossannah and Shyla at the castle.

We got there in the middle of the night. We chose a large house and knocked on the door. The woman who opened the door was ecstatic to let us in and showed us to two rooms. One was meant for Hector, and one was meant for the king and me. I opened my mouth to protest but the king held up his hand to quiet me. I remembered that to the rest of the world, we were married.

"I will sleep on the floor," he offered when the mistress of the house left us alone in the room.

"I don't mind the floor," I answered back. "It's kind of like the ground. The ground feels like home." He looked at me, thoughtfully. Then he climbed into the bed and fell asleep. I lay down on the floor and fell asleep as well.

In the morning he shook me awake and I followed him down to the family's dining room, where a crowd of about twenty people were seated. They reached and scooped and ate whatever they could get their hands on. We sat down with them and their actions quieted as they caught sight of us. I felt as if I was on display. No one said a thing.

A few moments went by in uncomfortable silence when Hector came down the stairs and took a seat next to me.

"Who are you today?" I asked matter-of-factly, not wanting to stray from my normal routine with him.

"Still just Hector," he said as he chuckled. "It's never going to change."

Yeah, right. I thought to myself. Then he noticed the painful tension as well.

It took Hector only seconds to figure out what to do. He reached out and grabbed a plate filled with bacon and began loading it onto his plate. This seemed to start a chain reaction and the group was back to its regular routine.

"These are your slaves," the king whispered to me. I looked at these people, seemingly normal, attacking the food before me. They didn't seem to be lacking for anything. They were clothed and some of them were on the heavier side so I knew that they were well fed. The only indication of their bondage came when the meal was over and the man at the head of the table started barking out orders as to what job they would be doing that day. They all got up and obediently went their own way.

"I would like to talk to some of them," I mentioned to the king and then spoke up to the man at the head of the table, who was also getting up to go and do some chore. "I would like to talk to some of them."

"I wouldn't say no to a queen," the man from the table smiled warmly. It still made me uneasy that so many people who didn't know me would give me my way so freely.

The slaves didn't have much to say. They only told me that they were happy with their work and didn't mind being a slave. I thought that it was odd that so many of them were so willing to be content with that sort of life, until I talked to a large, overgrown man that they called Thor.

"It's better for us to be slaves," Thor told me, "than to be out there starving. Some of us broke the law just so that we would have a place to sleep and food to eat." This made me very sad. At this point I decided that maybe the system that was in place was the best for everybody, but then I saw her.

She was only about six-years-old. She was small and fragile. She had shiny, strawberry blonde locks like Rossannah's and I instantly thought of her as Rossannah as a child. She was struggling with a large bucket filled to the brim with water. I watched her reposition the bucket many times to try to get it to the field where the thirsty workers were waiting. She'd take a couple steps and set it down, reposition herself, think it over, and then pick it up again. Take a couple steps, and then start the process all over again. She looked too frail to be out here.

"What was her crime?" I asked Thor, pointing to the child.

"She stole some bread for her family, two years ago," Thor sighed. "Poor thing was too young to know what freedom was like. Too bad, some young people actually do make things better for themselves, and she will never have the chance."

I stalked angrily over to the man from the head of the table, who was working alongside the slaves.

"I want that girl out of the fields!" I screamed, pointing at the small child. The little girl looked up from across the field, horrorstruck. This seemed to spark an ambitious bone in her body as she began straining herself to make better time with her bucket. I can only imagine what was going on in her mind across the field as she could only see, and not hear me, yelling at this man who was supposed to be her master while pointing at her and thrashing my arms around in her defense.

"She's fine," the man from the head of the table tried to assure me. "Look, my son's out here and he is the same age." He pointed in the direction of another child, a stocky little boy carrying another water bucket around the fields with ease.

"She is sickly looking!" I maintained. "She's obviously not cut out for this kind of work." The man looked at the little girl struggling and a deep realization seemed to hit him.

"I will send her to the kitchen with my wife," he conceded. "She can help prepare the meals from now on. That should be something she will be better suited for."

"No," I argued. "She is coming with me."

The farmer nodded his head to show that he understood. He headed across the fields to the little girl and I could see him explaining to her that she was going to come with me. She seemed to plead with him and I saw her start to cry in alarm. He soothingly put his hand on her shoulder and she quieted. He wasn't a bad man, I decided, just another victim of the way things were.

He brought the little girl to me. She looked at me with sullen and scared eyes. It was as if I was taking something away from her. I thought about changing my mind, but couldn't bring myself to do it.

"This is my home," she said to me, in tears. "Please don't take me away from my home."

"I will take you to your real home," I reassured her. "You will be back with your family." Her tears stopped instantly and her face lit up.

"May I pack my things?" the little girl said as she turned to the farmer. He nodded his approval. I discussed with the farmer where the little girl had come from so I could return her to her family. He seemed to be as grateful to get rid of her as she was to be going home.

The king and I took the little girl home together. It was a journey that took another day. Our carriage pulled up to a little shack that was falling apart. I began to wonder if there was anybody inside, when a crowd of thirteen children and two adults began to shuffle out of its tiny clutches. I wondered how a house this small could fit so many people.

I got out of the carriage first, followed closely by the king and then Hector. A moment or two went by before the little girl finally appeared and Hector gingerly helped her down.

Thirteen pairs of hands from the girl's siblings reached out to touch her, to embrace her. I looked up into the faces of her parents expecting relief and happiness but instead I found only sorrow and regret. I looked around at the meager reality of their existence and was instantly propelled into a need to do something. I approached the parents with purpose.

"The forest has plenty of resources, and people that will be willing to help you learn to use them if you mention my name," I explained. "Tell them that Joby sent you. Everybody will know who I am and that I sent you, but you have to use my name. Don't call me the queen."

The mother hugged me. It was clear that I had done more for her than anybody had ever done in her life. I decided that I would now take more of an interest in the lives of the people that I was supposed to rule. I turned around triumphantly to face the king. He didn't look too happy with me.

"You didn't have to send them to the forest," he fumed as we were heading back to the farm with the slaves. "I would have helped them. The key to keeping everybody together is their faith that you will do everything you can to make their lives better. You just sent them to someone else."

"Who says that everybody needs to be together?" I said, rolling my eyes at him.

"Those people will die of starvation before you get to them."

"Better than them starting a war with us."

The conversation was over. He knew that something had changed within me after that scene. He knew that it wasn't his world versus my world anymore. The lines between us had begun to blur together and I began seeing the people on both sides and had an intense need to change things for the better. The problem was that he already thought that things were as they needed to be.

As we headed toward the slave farm where we had left our belongings, I began to imagine ways that I could make the world better. I thought that punishing children in the same way that you would punish an adult was not a very effective way of keeping the peace. Nor was slavery an acceptable punishment. In my mind, it did two things: encouraged crime among the most impoverished because of the promise of a better life, and robbed people of their freedom for the rest of their lives for minor offenses. I thought that a reorganization of justice was in order. My thoughts carried me all the way toward the farm.

We got out of the carriage and made our way toward the house to collect our things. The king stood on one side of the room, and I busied myself on the other. Neither of us felt like speaking to the other.

The screaming started as one voice, angry
and maniacal, and then exploded into a
multitude of more terrified sounds. I stood
up and walked over to the window to see where
the sound was coming from and bellowed for the
king to follow me quickly as I turned to the
door and ran out to where Hector had wrestled
Thor to the ground and was forcing his face
into the mud.

"Hector, STOP!" I yelled at him as I
began pulling at his arms and shoulders. He
wouldn't budge.

"Mary! It's Mary!" The king reminded me.

"Mary, STOP!" I corrected myself. Aside
from a short pause at the recognition of the
name, Hector did not stop. We both began
pulling at him, but when he raged like this he
seemed to have superhuman strength.

Then, all of a sudden, Hector went slack.
He sat on Thor's back looking down at his
hands and around at the many people encircling
him in confusion. He suddenly stood up and
Thor rolled over, choking and spitting out the
mud he had wedged in his mouth.

"What happened?" Hector asked, shocked.
The time had come for us to tell Hector about
his problem. On the way back to the castle we
talked about it. For two days we discussed
what he was. I showed him my journal that I
had been keeping of his behavior. He made me
promise to show him after each episode.

When we returned, Hector excused himself
to his room, depressed about learning of his
condition. Shyla and Rossannah watched as he

scurried away without acknowledging them. They asked if he was someone else and we explained what had happened at the farm.

He didn't eat meals with us that day and the Hawk made reappearance. The next day he came back as cheerful and full of life as ever. He explained that since he didn't have any control over when he was himself he wanted to be as much like himself as possible when he could be. I liked that. I identified with it.

We had a whole week before there was any other incident. It allowed us to remember that Hector had good in him, although the bad was always there, forever looming around us. I wondered if it could ever be helped.

One day after that week, Rossannah and I were out in the fields for our walk when we saw Hector head out to the stables. I had noticed that the stable hand that had guarded me had left only moments earlier and that Hector was in there alone with the horses. I wanted to make sure that everything was alright so I told Rossannah that I wanted to go check it out.

"Let's go get the king first," she pleaded with me, "He has more experience with Hector than we do. He's stronger, too."

"You go ahead and get him," I ordered. "If he wants to hurt the animals or burn down the stables he could probably do it before you find him and get him here. I'm going in after him to try to distract him."

"Okay," Rossannah agreed. "Be careful."
I nodded and she ran off as I made my way
toward the stables.

When I got there I could hear him
throwing things around inside of the stables.
I heard the horses whinnying in surprise and
frustration and counted to three before
swinging open the stable doors to come face to
face with him. His hair was slightly
disheveled where he was clawing at it with his
hands. He looked at me with an irrational
gleam in his eye and continued on his
unprovoked rage, picking up pails and other
items and throwing them across the room. It
was as if he was fighting with himself for
control.

I carefully walked up to his writhing
body as he turned away from me and reached out
my hand to touch his shoulder, but before my
hand ever came in contact with the tattered
remains of his shirt, his body quieted.

He turned around to face me, eyes blank
and staring into the void above my head,
searching for something. Apparently what he
wanted to see wasn't there so he lowered his
gaze to my face and managed to beam at me with
a wide and friendly smile. He walked toward
me and reached out his hands to rest them
gently on my shoulder and looked into my eyes.
Then his grip tightened and his fingernails
dug deep into my arms.

"Hector, you're hurting me!" I complained
and batted him away. He reached his arms out

again and I slapped him in the face to bring him out of his trance. "Hector…STOP!"

A dark realization hit me as I realized that this was definitely not Hector, nor was it any of the other personalities that I had seen. The body language was deliberately threatening, its primary intention to strike fear in the intended victim. All of his other violent personalities were quick and attacked as a spur of the moment. This one was adamantly dragging out the process for added effect.

"Roman?" I asked horrorstruck.

He chuckled menacingly and I knew that I was in trouble. The king had told me that this was the only personality that I would have to worry about, but was confident that I would never see it. He had told me that he had only come out twice. I wondered what horrors Roman had in store for me. I decided that I didn't want to find out and turned to dash for the door.

I managed to make it to the still open stable door but was ripped back and thrown to the floor of the stables as he slammed it shut and then turned back to look down at me. He stood there staring at me for what seemed like a lifetime but lunged at me when I finally made the attempt to stand up and escape again. His hands were around my neck now and he was choking me with all of his strength. My hands fidgeted around for something to grasp so that I could attempt to knock him out but I found nothing. Then he stopped.

He stood up. I coughed and caught my breath, relieved that I was no longer with Roman, but that was a foolish supposition. I panted as I watched him pace back and forth in front of me and held out my hand for him to help me up. He looked at me and chuckled again and I realized that I was wrong and this was only part of my torture. It was going to come in waves.

I looked longingly at the door but knew that I would never make it there. I turned to look at him pleadingly, hoping that some part of Hector would come out and save me, and realized that he had exposed himself. He pounced on me a second time, one hand on my neck squeezing the life out of me, and the other fumbling with my dress, trying to pull it up. I know I should have been more concerned with the hand around my neck but I fought with him to keep my clothing in place.

"AAAAAHHHH!" He screamed into my face in frustration. I assume it was an attempt to unnerve me so that I would stop fighting, but it only increased my fervor to protect myself. He gave up on his attempt to disrobe me with one hand and removed his hand from my neck. I began to cough again and tried to roll my body to the side but he roughly slammed my back to the ground. He began to rip my dress in two from the top down and as my breasts fell out, exposed, I felt him mercifully being pulled off of me and cried out in appreciation as the king pinned Roman to the wall. Rossannah rushed to my side, crying out my name and I sat up as she folded her arms protectively around me and I pulled the now severed upper part of my dress together.

My guard appeared in the door and gasped at the scene in front of him. He quickly fetched some rope and helped the king tie the fidgety man into a chair. I imagined Hector as an outline. A shell of a body that could be shaded any color imaginable. He could be bright and filled with sunshine one moment, but then the black darkness could be poured into him and he could take anybody down at any moment. Black can cover any color, even the brightest ones.

After they had successfully immobilized him, the king disappeared into one of the stalls and came out with a horse blanket, which he wrapped around my shoulders to help me hide my uncovered breasts. I pulled it close around me and Rossannah and the king simultaneously helped me to my feet so that I wouldn't have to take my hands off the comforting blanket.

"Keep him here until you are sure he has reverted back to Hector," the king instructed my guard.

We walked back to the castle in complete silence. I wanted to say something, but couldn't find the words to say it. It was harder still to express what I wanted because I was standing beside the woman that I loved and so I just said "okay".

"Okay?" He replied in confusion and I looked up at him in a mixture of shame and purpose.

"Okay," I clarified hoarsely, "I understand the need for an heir. I agree." I felt Rossannah's hands drop from my back. I looked at her betrayed face and tried to flash her an apologetic glance without it being noticed by the king.

"I think you got it from here," she seethed, and stalked off in anger. I wanted to go after her but the weight of my responsibility was too great this time. I couldn't allow the lives of so many people to be in the hands of Hector if something were to happen to me.

CHAPTER 14

HEIRS AND ERRORS

"No!" Rossannah screeched at me from the corner of my room. "No, if you do this that's it. I will leave. I will go back to my father's house. I won't come around anymore."

"Rossannah, please," I pleaded. "I have to do this. You know what Hector is capable of. If I don't do this, one day he could be in charge of you, he could be in charge of the tribes, he could be in charge of everybody."

"No," Rossannah repeated again, folding her arms and shaking her head definitely.

"Rossannah," I whispered, searching for the words, "this is bigger than us."

I understood why Rossannah had a problem with this, but it wasn't as if I was going to enjoy what I was about to do. Her anger at me was just putting more stress on me than what I needed.

Rossannah threw her hands up in the air and stormed out of the room. I followed her into her own. She began to tear things out of her closet and throw them on the bed. I watched in horror.

"What are you doing?"

"Leaving," she replied. I wanted to argue with her. I wanted to stay there and keep her from going, but I knew that if I did the fate of everyone else was sealed.

"I hope you stay," I whispered and I walked out of the room, tears flowing down my cheeks. It was my only option because if I would have stayed for one more minute, I would have broken down. I had to sacrifice myself for the good of everyone.

The walk to the king's room was excruciatingly long and painful. It seemed to take a lot longer than it actually did. I knocked on the door and found myself wishing that it had taken much longer to arrive. He opened the door to find me there and invited me in.

We stood there awkwardly, not daring to look at each other. After a few moments he began to pace uncomfortably around, not sure what to do in the situation. He finally came to rest on a chair on the other side of the room from me. Good. He was making me nervous.

I found myself sitting down at the foot of his bed. Maybe he saw this as an invite, because he stood up and came to sit down beside me. I scooted myself a little farther away from him.

"How do we do this?" He asked me, genuinely confused.

"I don't know," I replied honestly, "I thought that you would be taking the initiative here."

"I really don't know how," he confessed. "I've never done this before. I mean...I know how...I just don't know where to start."

Two hours later I headed back to my own room, leaving him alone in his bed, asleep. I had gotten up, got dressed, and tiptoed out the door as fast as I could get out of there. On the way back to my room I bumped into Hector pacing the halls. He turned his face away from me as I approached him.

"I'm leaving in the morning," he said in embarrassment. I reached out and put a sympathetic hand on his cheek. I reached down into my pocket and brought out the journal that I had been writing and handed it over to him.

"This will help your family and friends control those people that you become," I explained as I handed over the little book.

"I'm sorry," Hector whispered as a tear rolled slowly down his cheek.

"You didn't hurt me," I smiled, feeling charitable. "Roman did. He's gone now." Hector burst into tears and hugged me. I was less than enthusiastic about the embrace and I think he felt it. He let go almost immediately and I flashed him a warm but careful smile. It was true that he couldn't seem to help his condition, but I knew the pain of not being able to tell when he was experiencing one of his episodes.

I left Hector quickly in the hopes that I could somehow escape the awkwardness between us. It would always be there now, even on the days where he was himself.

Before long, I was back at my room. I took a deep breath and opened the door.

Rossannah was sitting there on the foot of my bed, waiting for me, eyes staring at the floor in dismay. I stared at her in disbelief as she stood and walked over to me. She embraced me and I let go of the tears that I had been holding inside.

"How did it go?" Rossannah asked sullenly.

"I don't know," I sniveled, "it hurt at first, but then it was just uncomfortable. I don't think he noticed either way."

"Do you think it worked?" she said gently, rubbing my arm.

"I hope so," I cried, "I don't want to do that again." I took her hand and we both got into my bed and fell asleep. At this point, I didn't care who caught us together. I just wanted to be near her. Rossannah and I shared a room after that night, and nobody questioned us about it, although Shyla would throw dirty looks our way every once in a while.

We were all relieved to be informed a few months later that I was indeed pregnant. Shyla explained to me that it was very lucky I had become pregnant so fast. I agreed with her.

The king seemed to agree as well. For weeks we had been unable to look at each other during meetings and over meals. We had started eating on separate schedules just so that our interactions with each other were limited. It was a mutual understanding that we wouldn't even talk about it unless we were forced to do it again. Now that we were satisfied that we would never be required to relive that night, our relationship relaxed and our normal banter and arguments recommenced.

My new situation created a new annoying side effect. People had begun to treat me differently from all directions. The servants were the least of my problems. I had always been pampered and adored by them and was used to it. Pregnancy caused a slight increase in their attention to my care, which was hardly noticeable from what they had done before. Rossannah and Shyla fussed over me and demanded that I rest more. The walks in the fields with Rossannah became a thing of the past and I desperately missed them. The worst of them all, however, was the king. Before my pregnancy, he was content to let me be on my own whenever our coexistence was not required. Now the life growing inside me sparked his constant presence at my side. I couldn't turn around without him being there. I began to regret my decision to let this happen immediately.

It didn't take me long to reach my boiling point. It was the middle of the night and I was lying awake, staring at the glass of water on my bedside table, contemplating taking a drink from it. I didn't want to move and wake up Rossannah who slept so lightly that even if my body would shift slightly in my sleep it would wake her up in concerned grogginess. Tonight she had her arm around me as an added bonus to the possibility that she would wake up the second that I moved.

I heard footsteps in the hall that stopped at our bedroom door. I heard the creak of the hinges as it opened and light flooded the room. The king stood there staring down at me as if what he was doing was not in the least bit out of the ordinary.

"What are you doing in here?" I screamed as I got up to my feet. "Get out!"

"I'm sorry," he apologized, "I was just checking on you. I do it every night. Usually you are sleeping. I thought if you needed anything I could get it for you."

"Rossannah will get me anything I need," I yelled pointing at her. She was now sitting upright in bed with a look of horrified confusion on her face. "I do not need you checking on me."

The king turned around and hurried away. I turned back to the bed, but couldn't bring myself to lie back down. I walked across the room and sat down in the chair and wondered how many times he had been in my room.

"You need to sleep," Rossannah yawned and threw the covers off of her. She came over to me and coerced me to stand up and come back to the bed.

"Soon, we won't be able to sleep," Rossannah smiled as we stared at each other in the dark. "Let's take advantage of it now."

I reached out for her hand and we fell asleep, but it was an uneasy one for me. I couldn't get past the realization that the

king had known that Rossannah and I were
sharing a room, and a bed. It followed me
into my sleep as dreams painted all kinds of
scenarios as to how this could come back to
haunt me.

Over the next few nights I woke up
sporadically. My body seemed to be trying to
catch the king in the act once again. I
sometimes heard his footsteps in the hall.
They would stop beside my door for a moment or
two, but the door never opened again. Instead
they just walked away in the other direction
as quickly as they had come. Throughout my
pregnancy these sounds would wake me up, but I
became used to them.

Then one night, I welcomed that sound. I
was at the end of my pregnancy and Rossannah
had spent the night with her father because he
was on his deathbed. I was alone when the
pains started. For two hours I laid in bed,
unable to move as the pain came in waves, and
so tired in between that I would fall into a
deep sleep. Then they started to come closer
together and I didn't know what to do. I
screamed out for Shyla to come and help me,
but she either didn't hear or wasn't in bed
yet.

Then the familiar footsteps came and
landed behind my door. I cried out. He
knocked on the door first and I invited him
in. It was another one of those times where
the situation called for the unsettling trust
between us and he ran off to find someone to
help me with my labor.

Shyla was at my side moments later, stroking my hair and speaking to me soothingly. Rossannah appeared minutes after that. The time came for me to push and Shyla caught the baby girl as I clenched Rossannah's hand. She was dark like I was, but when she opened her eyes they mirrored the emerald in the king's and Rossannah's.

Then the labor pains began again and I gave birth to a second child. I did not see him right away and I heard Shyla gasp as she saw him. I asked her what was wrong and she looked at me with joyful tears.

"I hoped it was true," she laughed, "this entire time I guarded myself in case it wasn't really you. Now I know that it is." She held my son up to show me. My blonde, white son with the lion-shaped strawberry birthmark across his face: a genetic trait of the royal family.

After a few moments alone with Rossannah, Shyla, and my newborn children, the king was invited to come and see the babies. He could have said a million things about them, but what he chose to say was the least of what any of us thought that he would.

"Which one was born first?" he demanded hurriedly.

"The girl," Shyla informed him.

"We should tell people that it was the boy," he addressed me, "The boy with the birth mark of the first king. He should be the next ruler."

I was aware of the rules of first birth in the kingdom and considered this. I had foolishly assumed in the few moments that I had alone with them that they would be given equal station. I looked at the children symbolically and realized that one of them would have a great amount of freedom while the other would be trained to be a great ruler and decided that I would most like the girl to be free. She embodied most what I was. I agreed to the lie.

I named the boy Prince. It was a way for me to redeem myself from the lie and to expose him for what he was and should be forever. Even when he became the king one day, he would forever walk around with that name, hopefully keeping him humble long after I was no longer around to remind him of the truth. The girl I named True. I had robbed her of her position, but gave her a title to show that she was the true ruler of the land.

After the birth of my children, I noticed a difference in the amount of warmth that Shyla presented toward me. I no longer found her mechanical and distant. She was also a tremendous help with the babies. She told me that it was because they were symbolic on what she had missed out on and she was happy to have a small part in their lives.

As the children grew, we knew that we had made the right decision about the boy being the next leader. He was laid back and methodical, a perfect candidate for a student. The girl, however, was more like me. She was hard to control and spontaneous. The only person that could seem to rein her in at all was Rossannah. *She was just like me.*

CHAPTER 15

LONG FORGOTTEN PLANS

Five years passed. I had finally managed to convince people that slavery was wrong. We were now squabbling over a justice system and what appropriate punishments were for certain crimes. The king seemed to think that all crime warranted the most severe of punishments, but I disagreed. I simply wanted to form a system where one day, people would take care of themselves with minimal help from a leader. It was better for everyone, especially my son who would be forced to give up aspects of his life that I didn't think he should have to. The king disagreed with my belief system. He claimed that people needed someone to show them how to behave. In the forests, we called those people parents, but then we grew up and knew how to behave.

People stopped coming to the councils after a few shouting matches between the king and me. I guess nobody likes to watch two grown people squabbling about how we are all going to live our lives. I know that I would feel angry if I had to watch others decide my fate when I should be able to decide it for myself. Maybe that isn't the case for some people though. Maybe some people just want peace.

We had spent another extremely stressful afternoon once again yelling at each other in an empty room, except for the elderly men that always showed up at the head table around us. The king had stormed off again in one of his fits about how he had been trained on all of this and that his way was for the better. There had been three generations of royalty to prove it. I had mentioned that there had been many generations of tribes as well in the forest, and they were doing just as well. I heard the old man who always sat beside me chuckle as the king slammed the door behind him.

"He understands what he is supposed to do," the old man giggled, "but he's never understood why he is supposed to do it."

"Excuse me?" I asked perplexed.

"You, on the other hand," the man continued, "don't know what you are supposed to do, but you understand why you are supposed to do it. I thought that the two of you together would be able to figure it out. I guess I was wrong. Perhaps it is time for me to intervene."

"I don't understand what you are talking about," I frowned.

"When he was young," the man explained to me patiently as the other old men in the room leaned in to listen, "he was trained on how to be a good leader. He was told how to punish someone, how to act mercifully while at the same time being stern enough to command loyalty, and how to make laws that would benefit the majority of the population. As he grew, he was trained on how to keep the society together. It was all part of a greater plan. When it came time for him to learn the lesson that would teach him the point of it all, his teacher died. All he could do was rule by the way he had been trained. He had no understanding of why he had been taught to do the things that he did, and that he was meant to take the next step."

"The next step to what?" I asked, intrigued.

"The plan to help us all grow up," the old man informed me. "I think it's going to have to be you."

"I'm sorry," I apologized, "I still don't understand what it is that you want me to do."

"What is the one thing that you want more than anything, even though you have gotten used to the way things are and seem comfortable enough?" he asked me. I thought for a moment.

"Freedom," I answered him. His eyes sparkled and he tapped his nose to show that I had answered him right.

"You see," he explained again, "you have the answer, but he has the question. He is primarily concerned with leading everybody into a better life, but he doesn't yet understand that he can't provide it all. He can't have all the answers. People have to figure those out for themselves. His job has always been to be the next person in a long line of people to slowly change the mindsets of everybody so that they would have the ability to think for themselves without killing each other over it. We were all brought into this world as children, but we must grow up eventually. Sadly, he was never given the chance to learn that lesson. In fact, he fights it. You, however, have had the opportunity to learn it from birth."

I started to become frustrated. I had no idea what he was talking about and it must have shown on my face. He smiled at me reassuringly, letting me know that I would understand in time.

"I want to show you something," he said, producing a sheet of paper and handing it to me.

"What is this?" I asked, as I took it from his hands and began to read.

"It was called the Bill of Rights," he explained. "When I was a child it was no more than a fairy tale, but it held some significance at one point. Not enough people cared about it to keep it alive, I guess. I'm still learning about the world that produced it because nobody alive has ever lived in it."

"How are you learning about it if nobody has lived in it?"

"Books," he replied. "It's difficult sometimes. Sifting through and trying to find the ones that are filled with facts, and separating those that are packed with nonsense. Not to mention that they are old and falling apart and some of them are missing large chunks. Still, we have people out there that are copying and recopying them to keep them together. There is a whole library of them in the west, beyond all of the kingdoms. The west kingdom is sort of a refuge for everybody that can't stomach the rules of the rest and they welcome strangers there."

"I know," I announced, "I told someone to go there once." I sighed as I remembered Joseph.

"We will go there when you are ready," he offered. I looked at him doubtfully.

"How do you know that I will ever be ready?" I asked.

"You will know, and that is how I will know," he promised.

"What is your name?" I asked, realizing that I had referred to him as "the old man" for years, and I suddenly had a desire to address him. It was as though he had suddenly become my father.

"Gage," he smiled at me warmly.

"It's nice to finally know your name," I smiled back at him. He acknowledged my warmness by nodding his head. Then he stood up and walked out of the room, followed by the rest of the old men. I thought about following them. I was now curious as to where they went. I never saw them around the town, and they definitely did not live in the castle. I decided not to follow them, though. Something told me that they needed their refuge.

I sat in the completely empty room for a long time, pondering what Gage had told me. I wanted to understand everything that he and I had discussed, but I was still lacking in some forms of knowledge that the king had been taught from birth. I got a bad taste in my mouth when I thought about working together with him, but at this time I realized that it was the only way for us to both realize what we were supposed to know all along. I decided to seek him out. I left the room in a hurry to look for him.

"I need to talk to you," I said urgently when I caught up with him in one of the gardens. "It's important."

"You will not listen to reason," he countered. "I have nothing to say to you." He started to walk away. I reached out and grabbed his arm. He stiffened, and then softened. He turned around to face me.

"What is it you want?" He looked at me accusingly.

"I just want to try an experiment with you," I answered. "Nothing big, I just want you to come into the forest with me and trust in whatever I say. Two weeks. We can have the men at council run everything for a while. It will teach us to work together." He glanced at me suspiciously.

"Rossannah probably wouldn't like it," he countered.

"Rossannah will understand," I disagreed, "she always does." I had my doubts but didn't let them show.

"Fine," he reluctantly agreed, "When do we leave?"

"Tomorrow," I replied, "I'll tell Rossannah tonight. You can inform the men from council."

"I can't. I don't know where they live." The king sighed. I scowled. I had assumed that he would know.

"We'll have to tell them at the next council," I replied, "then we will go right after."

It took surprisingly very little to convince Rossannah that to go into the forest alone with the king wouldn't be a mistake. Shyla, on the other hand, was not so easy to pacify with words. She begged me not to go and to stay in the safety of the castle. As the king and I walked into the forest on the appointed day, Rossannah and the Hawk held the screaming woman back as she called out my name and tried to break free to get to me. I couldn't blame her for her concern. I was a little apprehensive myself.

We walked for a day and a half, only stopping to eat the food from our sack that was prepared for us by the servants. We stopped completely when the food was gone.

"What do we do now?" The king asked me, clearly concerned over his lack of food. He had never been in this position before, but it was something that I had planned out.

"We get our own food," I replied. I gathered some materials and told him to watch me to learn how to make a bow and arrows. Then I told him to do the same. It took him a long time to get it right and it was dark before he had a useable product, but that was fine with me. He was learning and that was all part of my plan.

"I'm hungry," he complained, "where is the nearest town? I'd like to get something to eat."

"We just left it," I explained. "We are going to get ourselves something to eat. It's hard to hunt in the dark. We'll have to find some fruit." He followed me around the trees and pointed out trees with little berries here and there. I had to explain to him they were poisonous and he sighed heavily every time. We finally managed to find a clearing with a line of raspberry bushes surrounding it.

"You can eat those," I told him, pointing out the berries. He rushed to the bushes gratefully and began stuffing himself.

"These are good!" he exclaimed, juice running down his greedy chin. "I've never had anything like this. We should have people come and gather these."

"Or we can come out here and gather them ourselves," I mentioned, "That way we could get as many as we wanted and wouldn't have to rely on other people. They might spoil by the time they would get to us."

"Oh," he frowned, "I didn't realize."

"We will hunt tomorrow," I announced. I picked a couple of berries and ate them. Then I built a fire to keep away the wild animals and lay down beside it. I was tired after walking all this time without rest. I fell asleep within a few minutes.

When I woke up, the king was lying beside me, painfully close. I was stunned at his proximity and the fact that I hadn't noticed it in the night. I stood up and walked around the ring of rock and pile of ashes that had been our fire last night and sat down on the other side. He stirred and woke up seconds after the warmth of my body had left him. He sat up and smiled at me like a silly little baby, red raspberry juice still staining his face.

"Get the bow and arrows you made," I ordered him forcefully, "I'm going to teach you to hunt today."

I didn't realize how hard it would be to teach somebody to hunt with a bow and arrow. I found a new respect for Sheena as I watched the king miss every animal he aimed for. After a couple of hours, I decided to shoot a rabbit to ensure that we would have something to eat that night. Then I went back to teaching him how to do it. I remembered that Rossannah had a hard time adjusting to the forest as well.

We ate my rabbit that night. The next night we ate another that I had shot. For two weeks we had my rabbit kills. Then it came time for us to go home.

"One more night," he pleaded with me, "I can do this. I just need one more night." I reluctantly agreed, thinking I had failed in my mission and that he would never be able to shoot anything.

I was wrong. The next morning I watched him spend an hour making error after error. I eventually just gave up on giving him instruction and sat down on a fallen tree, waiting for him to decide that he had enough. He didn't want to make that decisions I stood up to try to convince him that it wasn't a big deal that he couldn't hunt. As I approached him, a doe walked out of the trees and into our sight. We both stared at it in awe for a moment or two, marveling in its beauty. Then I saw him slowly raise his bow and pull back the arrow.

The arrow hit the deer in the neck and it immediately fell to the ground. I looked at him astonished. He had a surprised look on his face, which eventually changed into one of pride and excitement.

"I did it!" he exclaimed to me and then embraced me. "I actually killed something.

"Let's cut it up and carry it home," I said stiffly, uncomfortable with his entrapment. He dropped his embrace and looked at me questioningly, as if he didn't understand why I didn't act like he accomplished the greatest feat ever.

"Okay," he responded dejectedly.

We butchered the deer and put it in our two large food sacks to take home and began the long walk home. It was very lucky that it was a cold day or the meat might have spoiled on our way home.

"Why did you have me do this?" he wondered as we walked along.

"I wanted you to see how satisfying it is to be independent," I answered him. "I would think you would want that same satisfaction for your people."

"I guess I would," he agreed. "You're right." We walked along in silence for a while.

"Joby?" he addressed me. "I wouldn't have been able to experience that without you."

"What?" I asked, turning to him.

"I needed you to teach me to hunt. I couldn't do it on my own. I would have never ventured out into the forest unless you had suggested it. I would have never learned to make a bow or arrow without you. I couldn't have shot an animal in my lifetime if you didn't show me how. I needed you. Even my own father couldn't have taught me how to do that. Don't you think that people need someone to show them the way?"

This was it. I now understood what Gage had been trying to convey to me. I had gone into the forest trying to teach the king a lesson, and I had gotten one in return. It was true that freedom was a great reward for people, but they needed to be taught how to use it in the right way so that they didn't end up destroying themselves in the process. The king and I were now on the same track. Our new goal was to teach people how to strive for independence after they were able to safely achieve it.

"This could take a while," I sighed.

CHAPTER 16

READY

We returned to the castle with a newfound respect for one another. There was still no amicability between us, but we were now able to discuss our plans without ripping each other's heads off because they both pointed toward a common goal.

"I'm ready," I told Gage after a council meeting one day. I knew that I could leave and not worry about the king making any rash decisions while I was away.

"I know," he astounded me. He was so wise; he seemed to know before I did whatever the situation.

We left after a week. The king promised me that he wouldn't make any decisions without me. I believed him. He seemed to be a lot happier now that we had come to a mutual understanding about the world.

It took a long time to get where we were going. We crossed rivers and mountains and a long windy plain that seemed to go on forever. Then we arrived in the west kingdom.

"This is what life should be like," Gage informed me as we walked through rows of little houses. People stopped and greeted us warmly and wanted to know our stories. I felt love from people I had never met.

"Joby?" I heard the familiar, yet slightly deeper voice call out to me. "Is that you?" I turned around to stare straight into the face of my childhood friend, River. He had aged gracefully and didn't look much different from the boy I knew at age 16.

"River!" I cried and wrapped my arms around him.

"I can't believe it's you!" he cried out and we took a little time to catch up while Gage stood waiting patiently. I found out that River had been caught during the ambush, but for some reason they wanted to keep him alive. He had been a slave for two years before managing to escape and make his way to the west. He had gotten married and had a son the same age as my children.

River offered to let us stay with him at his house but Gage spoke up and told him that we still had a long way to go. He mentioned the library and River nodded knowingly.

"You are in for a treat," River smiled at me. "I learned to read in that library. I still need a little help, but I know enough."

Then we went on our way. It was two days away from the west kingdom. We came upon a large stone building in the middle of the night surrounded by a tall stone wall. It was built like a fortress and seemed impenetrable. Gage explained to me that it was like that because if it was ever destroyed, we would lose a lot of valuable information.

Gage hollered loudly at the large metal gate that barred the way into the huge complex. A moment later, a man appeared on the other side, asking us why we were there. Gage explained that he was there to train me to be a better leader and the gate was unlocked and swung open, allowing us to make our way inside. It was firmly shut behind us.

The man who had answered Gage at the gate lead us to two rooms, which he explained were ours until we left. I lay down on the bed and went to sleep immediately. Gage woke me up the next morning and I followed him into a large room filled with people copying words into fresh books and then putting them on shelves.

"Look around," Gage whispered to me, "but don't disturb anybody. They are doing important work. If you read something you like, let me know. I will talk to the big man here and he will have someone make you a copy."

I took in everything I could for three days, and I found some things that I really liked. I fingered through old books, magazines, and newspapers. I found a few diaries written by hand by people who lived before I was born. I learned a lot about the world before.

"There is one more thing that I need to show you," Gage approached me after the third day. "I haven't been back there in a while. It was my childhood home."

We walked for a few days again. Gage seemed to be getting more tired as we journeyed on. I began to worry about him, and asked if he wanted to go back. He told me that I needed to see what he wanted to show me. It would help me understand.

"But don't the people at the library take trips here to find more books and other written articles?" I argued with him. "I could wait until they do and come back with them."

"I need to be here with you," he explained patiently, "What you need to know, nobody else can tell you about this place. Nobody else is old enough to remember. I think I am the oldest person alive now. I haven't heard from my sister in a long time."

It was fuzzy at first when I saw it. I wasn't sure what I was looking at. Then as we walked closer it began to take form. There were buildings for as far as I could see, all kissing the sky. It looked like a metal and stone forest, beckoning us into it.

We approached the first building and Gage motioned me inside. I opened the door to a little house, smaller than the buildings in the middle.

"These were rare." Gage informed me. "They were only built on the outskirts of the city. They were for police and their families to help keep people in the city."

I walked through the little house, staring at glass from the broken windows. I came to a little bedroom door and opened it. I gasped at the sight of two skeletons lying on a dusty bed surrounded by cobwebs and debris. I turned around to face Gabe who was two steps behind me.

"It's this way in every building," he informed me. "The skyscrapers are worse. It smelled awful here when everything was rotting. Now there is just nothing left."

"What happened?" I whispered, feeling myself tearing up.

"War. Disease. Starvation." he spoke out as if reading off a numbered list. "You name it. A classic example of what happens when people rely too much on the government and then the government disappears."

"Why didn't they try to help themselves?" I asked, incredulously.

"Some of them did," Gage explained. "And that is why there is still a human race. But we are going extinct. There are not a lot of us left. But you and your husband have just taken the first step in making sure that we don't repeat our mistakes and destroy ourselves. Now it is up to you to try and correct the other ones as well. When you are teaching, make sure they are the right lessons."

"I don't know how to do that," I said. "I don't even know what they are."

"Look around the library," he smiled, "and read the history books. Copy them and bring them back with you. Put two and two together, and don't make the same mistakes. I'm too old now. I didn't do my part when I should have. I let others who were less experienced make the decisions when I should have been there all along."

We stood there staring into the room of death and I made a promise to myself that I would never let this happen. These people were never even buried.

"There is one more place that I would like to go," Gage said to me after our few moments of silence. "Would you come with me?"

"Yes," I agreed.

"It's in the middle, which is a little run down," he warned me. "So be careful." I followed him for what seemed like hours and stared up at the huge buildings that never seemed to stop climbing into the sky. Gage had informed me that each one of them used to house thousands of families.

"Here it is." Gage stopped in front of one of them. "We will have to take the stairs, I hope it is still stable enough to support us."

We walked up ten flights of stairs and Gage lead me to "his apartment door." We opened it to find two skeletons sitting on a couch, holding onto each other like the vines of very strange trees clinging to each other in the forest. I cringed at the sight but it seemed to have no effect on Gage.

"These were my parents," Gage mentioned, a little sadly. "My sister and I watched them get sick and die. Then someone came and got us. I don't remember them too well, but my sister could tell you some stories about them,

if you were to ever meet her. I don't know
why we never got sick."

He took me through, room by room,
explaining to me what some of the strange
things were that I had never seen before.
Radio. Television. Lamp. He explained
electricity and that we weren't able to find
any books on it to help us reproduce it.

Then he shuffled me into a little back
room filled with pictures of animals like
deer, rabbits, raccoons, and all of the
wildlife that I was used to seeing in the
forest. It seemed out of place in this world
that I had entered with him. It was a child's
room. *His* room.

He walked over and lay down on the bed
that was too small for him. His legs dangled
over the edge and he brought them up to
crumple himself into a little ball.

"Can you find your way back?" he asked
me, drowsily.

"What do you mean?" I gasped. "Why?"

"I'm going to die here tonight," he said,
matter-of-factly, "with my parents. I
would've liked my sister to be here as well,
but you can't always have what you want."

"I'm not going to leave you here," I
argued.

"I want to be here," he smiled softly at
me. "This was my home. I remember some good
things about this place. It was filled with
love. After all the disaster this is where I
want to spend my final moments of life."

"Then I am going to stay with you until you pass," I whispered. I couldn't imagine why someone would want to be here, in this metal graveyard when they could die somewhere much more beautiful. I realized at that moment that every individual has their own sense of what beauty is and nobody should try to take that away from them.

He slipped away quietly into the night. I watched over him and held his hand as he took his last breaths and went vacant. I thought about burying him but knew that it probably wouldn't be what he wanted, so I just let him lie on that bed alone for eternity before walking out of that city forever. I never wanted to return to it ever again.

I made my way back to the library and spent weeks finding what I needed to bring back with me. I copied them down fervently and by the time I left I had a wagon full of books that had to be pulled by a horse. I went into the west kingdom to work for the horse, but River refused to let me and gave me one of his.

Now I was ready to fulfill the promise that I had made to myself, and to the man that I had come to think of as my father. I was going to start a school for all of the children in my kingdom.

CHAPTER 17

THE SCHOOL

"You want to do what?" The king looked at me incredulously. "You can't do that. Decisions have to be made. Things have to be figured out. I can't do this without you. I don't know how to teach independence. You don't have time to teach kids to read and write and do all of that."

"I'm trying to teach independence," I explained, patiently. "It will be easier to teach it to the kids so that when they grow up they can take over. If they know how to read and write they can learn history and science. Read those books that I brought. You will know what I am talking about then."

"I don't have time to read those books. I have a responsibility here," he exclaimed.

We were back to our old argument about responsibility. He always seemed to think that I was always throwing mine away and that he had to pick up the extra slack. I doubted that was ever going to change.

"Just read the damn books," I spat and walked away from him. I decided to go outside and search for a place that would work as a site for a school. People looked at me curiously as I gazed around. There had been rumors as to why I had been gone so long.

People thought that I might be sick and didn't want anyone to know.

I decided on a spot that was not really suitable for planting but would be flat enough to put a building on. I wasted no time searching out the men responsible for construction of buildings and explained to them what I wanted. They began to work immediately and for once I was happy that I could get them to do anything I wanted without question.

The king was stubborn. He complained every chance that he got about my school project and refused to read the books that I had brought home. Instead, he began to come up with other projects that he thought were much more important and tried to get me involved in them. He became frustrated when I refused to give up on the school.

The school was completed within a week. It was just a little building with one room, but I knew from my reading that they all started out that way. Eventually, I could see it growing into something amazing, opening new realms of possibilities for everyone who entered it. For the first time ever I could breathe inside a building as I could out in the woods.

I walked around the town, letting everyone know that I wanted students to come to my school so that I could teach them how to read and write. Parents shook me off like I was trying to peddle them rat poison. I heard the same argument everywhere I went. They needed the children to help out with chores. I pushed harder.

The day that my school was opened I sat in the front of the room in my desk, looking around at the emptiness that had been perfectly sculpted to resemble what I had seen in picture books. The only thing missing was children.

It happened every day that way. I came to the little school and sat for hours, waiting for someone to show up. I felt myself die a little inside as time went on. I decided that in the end, I would bring my own children there and begin to teach them, even though the Hawk had been in charge of their education all this time.

It was soon very clear to me as I sat True and Prince on my lap and tried to instruct them, that I had no idea how to teach this kind of stuff. It was different than teaching someone out in the wilderness. I became frustrated with my children very easily when they wouldn't pay attention or got something wrong. I decided that I couldn't do this on my own, so I invited Rossannah to help me.

Rossannah was a new reader. She had only been reading for a year when I asked her to come and help me, but she was patient and kind with Prince and True and that is what I had needed. She seemed to be able to explain things in ways that I never could, and I stood back and watched her. I was a little ashamed of myself that Rossannah had a better relationship with my children than I had, but I was not built like she was. She had been born to be a mother.

True and Prince were young and learned faster than Rossannah. At some point, we both had to admit that she could not teach them anymore because she was still learning herself. I swallowed my pride and asked the Hawk to step in. She gladly accepted the job. She had missed working with the children. I had to explain very carefully that the lessons she was teaching them had to do with reading and writing skills only. I didn't want a repeat of what I had to go through. Rossannah also hung around for the Hawk's lessons and seemed to be doing a lot better with her work than when I had been teaching her.

The Hawk became an unlikely ally to us in the school argument. She managed to convince the king to stop fighting the issue. She seemed to be truly happy in her new role as teacher, and the children flourished under her instruction.

The three of us split up the workload when it came to the school. Rossannah worked to keep it clean and prepared food that she brought to the school, even though my children were the only students. I supervised the physical activities that we did to break up the day. The Hawk was responsible for the education. We were a well-organized team.

One day, we were all sitting around listening to the Hawk read the children "*Little Red Riding Hood*". I caught a glimpse of something through the corner of my eye and glanced over to see two children staring intently through the window. They ducked when they noticed that I had caught sight of them.

I got to my feet and left the school. I walked around the corner to where the window was and saw them sitting down under it, arguing with each other about what to do next.

"Come on in," I invited them. They stared at each other, terrified. "There's nothing to be afraid of, just come in and sit for a while."

The both got to their feet. The older one looked at me for a moment and I couldn't tell if he was going to run away. The little girl beside him grabbed him by the hand and it seemed to trigger a reaction in him. I laughed to myself as I saw them disappear into the schoolhouse. I stood out there for a moment or two, allowing myself to cry a few tears of joy before following them inside.

Rossannah grinned at me as she walked to my side and we both stared down at the two new children sitting on the floor beside my own, wide-eyed and eager, as they listened to the Hawk's story. After it was finished, the Hawk set the book down and asked the children questions that were deliberately designed by the three of us to make the children think for themselves. The two new children seemed to catch on fast and I felt better about the school and the world itself. They were the hope that I had held out for, that someone out there was willing to take steps to a better life.

A few days went by and the children showed up every day to learn. After that, other children began to trickle into the school, one by one. Then it came in a flood. We had to adjust our teaching plans because there were so many children showing up. Rossannah took over the new learners, teaching them what she could before turning them over to the Hawk. I took children in groups out to the woods and taught them hunting and foraging skills and organized races and other things so that the Hawk and Rossannah wouldn't be overwhelmed by their numbers. The children that had been there the longest were given "buddies" that they were responsible to help teach.

Months passed and the school had become much more successful than any of us had hoped. Then the adults started to trickle in. We decided that it would be best for everybody if we started to teach at night as well. Eventually, nearly the whole town showed up for lessons at least some of the time.

The king became increasingly more agitated as I spent more time at the school. He was beginning to see its importance but his complaint was that he felt like he was forced to rule alone. Now that he felt that there was a way out of his chains of responsibility, he resented me for spending so much time out of mine. It was as if he thought that I was putting more of a burden on him.

"I don't see why you can't spend a little more time helping me with the council," he fumed, "You are never there anymore. You never used to skip it. Now you spend all of your time at that school."

"I never used to skip it," I explained, "because I didn't think I would be able to trust you. I was there simply for the protection of my people and myself. I felt if I let you run things alone you would make life very hard for me."

"I just don't see why you have to be there every day!" he yelled, frustrated. "Progress doesn't have to happen overnight. You can let it take some time."

I agreed to spend three days a week helping him in council, which I now found extremely boring since we spent most of the time agreeing on things. We were both working toward a common goal and that made things less abrasive.

I convinced the king to come help me at the school a couple of days a week as well, although most of the time he was there he spent sitting in the back reading the advanced history books that we had not been able to introduce yet. Every once in a while he would stand up and walk over to me to point out something that he had read. I would nod and explain to him as he repeatedly pointed things out that I had read all the books. Then we would talk about whatever had excited him for a moment or two and he would go back to reading. He was almost as eager to learn as the children were.

Then he became the history teacher. He would come to the school for one hour every day to talk about something that he had read. It was amazing to watch him teach. He was animated and enthusiastic about the material that he talked about. He would act out battles and speeches and the children would cheer him on and beg him to borrow them the history books. He would gingerly hand them to the children, who would open the book and become frustrated with the words and then turn the book over to him again. Then he would begin talking again and the children would be mesmerized by his words and forget the disappointment that they had just suffered. He ignited a passion in the children that kept them coming to the school so that one day they might be able to pick up those books that he brought to life for them and devour every last word.

Years passed and some of the children that we had been teaching had learned just enough to go off to different towns and start their own schools. Some chose to stay and learn as much as they possible could. My children were ever present even as the hit their teen years and were supposed to be learning the more delicate matters of ruling. I had expected the Hawk to whisk them away at this time to teach them how to act "properly", but she seemed more committed to the school than ever before.

It didn't dawn on me that what we were
doing at the school was working until Prince
and True were 15-years-old. The children were
outside playing a game of football which they
had read about in one of the books that I had
recently brought back during my last trip.
True had gotten the ball and was running for
the touchdown when one of the boys caught up
to her and tackled her. True had let out a
scream of pain and I forced myself to stay
back as I watched Prince run up and pull the
large boy off of her.

"You are done playing!" he ordered the
large boy, pointing his finger to direct the
boy away from the group.

"I'm just doing what the rules say to
do!" the boy argued back. "I didn't do
anything wrong."

"I'm the future king!" Prince maintained.
"I say to leave and never come back."

"I don't have to listen to you," the boy
argued. "You aren't king yet, and even when
you are, I might not listen to you. They do
have voting now, you know. I'll just get
everybody on my side."

The large boy reached down and offered
his hand to True, who took it, and he helped
her up. True and Prince stared after the boy
as he stalked away and I noticed something in
True's face that I would have recognized
anywhere. It was the same look that I caught
Rossannah giving me on those days when we had
first started out. It was desire. True was

in love with this boy and I knew it was for his independence.

Prince seemed to convey a different emotion on his face as he glared at him. He had been humiliated. I realized that Prince was going to have a hard life. He was being raised to be a leader, but with the progress that we were making already I doubt that he would ever be able to claim that title. I began to understand what had prompted the king to be so rigid in his early life. He had taken control when he was the same age that Prince was now. He had not been given the opportunity to grow like Prince was going to have.

CHAPTER 18

FRIENDSHIP

I had spent a lot of years being at odds with the king, but now that I was forty, I felt that the time had come to forgive him for the years of blame that I had placed on him. I felt that the first step to doing this was to come to him with a problem that I would normally bring to Rossannah.

For fifteen years we had ignored the fact that we had children together, passing messages between the Hawk and Rossannah as a means of communicating what our roles should be with each child. I partnered with Rossannah to discipline and raise the children, and he partnered with the Hawk. We labored to keep our paths from crossing.

Today was different. I could have brought this problem to Rossannah and we could have sat the children down and talked to them together, but I wanted to build a bridge and so I sought him out.

I found him at the castle library, consuming one of the books that he had recently found himself on *his* latest trip to the west, which was becoming a regular thing for him as well. It was a romance novel. He was strangely intrigued by them. He had tried to pass one off to me, but I couldn't make it through the first chapter.

"I think that we better talk," I stammered, not entirely sure how to start a conversation with him that didn't involve making decisions for a thousand other people. "True and Prince are fighting."

"And you came to me?" He put down his book and raised his eyebrow. "This must be pretty bad."

"It's not that bad, really," I sighed, "I just thought you should know about it. I don't really think there is anything that we could do to fix it."

"What's going on?" He smiled widely and leaned forward in his chair to show that I had his full attention.

"True has a crush on this boy, Tommy," I began, slowly. "Prince hates him. He is accusing True of bringing down her family with this guy. I don't know where he is getting ideas like that."

"I'll talk to him," the king promised. "Maybe there is something we don't know about this kid."

"This kid stands up to Prince," I blurted out.

"Oh." The king sat back, thinking meticulously. He was quiet for a moment or two and then looked up at me with realization on his face and grinned from ear to ear. "That's great!"

"I know!" I exclaimed. "But we got to make Prince see that this is a good thing as well."

"I think we should probably talk to True about this boy, too," the king burst out as I turned to leave the room, "for her own safety."

"What are you talking about?" I twirled around. "I don't think she's in any danger from having a crush."

"Maybe not," the king answered back, "but I found this book while I was rummaging through some of the more entertaining books and I think you should read it."

He handed me a thick book that still smelled of fresh ink. It had obviously been transitioned very recently.

"All this time I have been worried about encouraging population growth," he explained to me, "Maybe that was a mistake. There have been a lot of unexplained deaths around here lately and I have my suspicions that some of the things in that book might be to blame."

"What is this?" I asked.

"It's a health book," the king explained. "They've just found it. I had to wait for them to transcribe it twice before I could take it. Apparently, sex can kill you."

I cringed at the word casually thrown out. It wasn't something that I was comfortable talking about with anybody but Rossannah. I placed the book back in his hand and turned to leave.

"I'm serious!" he urged and I stopped. He stood up and walked around me until we were standing face to face. He placed the book firmly in my hand.

"Read it," he ordered. "I read those books that you brought home. I know I resisted at first, but I read them and you were right. You have to read this, and then we have to bring it to the school. I know that I am right on this. If we ever want to accomplish this idea of independence that you are so fond of, we have to have people around to do it."

I grudgingly took the book and stalked away from him. I went to my room and planted it on my bedside table. Then I left it there, convinced it was another abomination like the romance novel that he had tried to get me to read.

That night as Rossannah and I were lying down, I picked it up to skim through it, but found myself engrossed in the science. As Rossannah leaned over me to blow out the candlelight that I was reading by, I waved her away and continued to read into the night as she fell asleep and dreamed beside me.

"You were right," I conceded to the king that morning at breakfast. "We do need to warn people about these things. I can't do it, but it needs to be done."

The first thing that we did was bring the book to the healer in town. Then we organized a mandatory class for all of the people of sexual age in town. It wasn't well received at first and we noticed that several of the people didn't seem to want to listen, but after a while we had gotten all of their attention.

It was too late to help the people who had already gotten sick, we didn't have enough information to cure them yet, but we were able to prevent others from getting sick. It wasn't anything that we had found in the book, it was something new, but there was no doubt in anybody's minds that it was caused by intercourse. Not a single virgin had caught the disease, and those that had been faithful and had faithful partners were also clean.

The success of catching and containing a problem together brought the king and me closer together. We started spending time together for enjoyment rather than out of necessity. I had spent most of the last five years consumed with the school and reading for education purposes. I had rarely spent any time in the forest anymore. The king began to help me out of that mindset that had trapped me for so long. We read books together and then discussed them. We hunted in the forest together. We even took trips to the west to bring back more books together.

Rossannah was disturbed by my sudden friendship with the king. I understood her discomfort. If I had been in her position I would have felt the same way. The truth was I liked having somebody around who reminded me that life could be fun, and Rossannah didn't do that anymore. I still loved her with all of my heart, but we had grown together and had become so rooted that there was never any room to take one foot out of the tree we had climbed into. I just needed someone to come along and help me out of that tree sometimes.

The school had a lot more helpers since the children who had started it were older and so I wasn't needed as much. I started leaving early and skipping days so I could spend time doing things that I had felt I had missed out on in my childhood. The king often accompanied me.

One day I decided to leave school to meet up with the king and Rossannah caught me by the arm. She begged me to stick around and help her with some of the children. I was particularly frustrated that day and refused. She let go dejectedly and I stalked away, upset with her without knowing why.

I walked through the castle, making my way to the library when I realized that there were footsteps approaching me from behind. I turned around to scold Rossannah for following me but was surprised to see the Hawk standing there.

"Joby," she whispered, urgently, "I need to talk to you now, before you get yourself into big trouble that you won't be able to dig yourself out of." She held out her hand to me and I took it nervously, not knowing what I was about to face. She led me to the council room where Rossannah, Shyla, and Ashlee were waiting for us.

"What's going on?" I looked around the room, confused. "What are you all doing here? Who is running the school?"

"Don't worry," the Hawk reassured me, "It's taken care of. We all came here because we are all worried about you."

"I'm alright," I scowled.

"You need to stop spending so much time with my son," the Hawk said forcefully, "You are giving him hope and that is not good for you or for him."

"What? We are friends," I answered. "He knows that. He knows that is all that we will ever be."

"No, he doesn't!" Ashlee cried out mournfully. "I've heard him talking to himself about you."

"He's always been in love with you," the Hawk announced. "I've tried to help him get over it, but he is trapped in this fantasy that you will eventually feel the same."

"And I know for a fact that you could never return those feelings," Shyla stared into my eyes. "I've told these women that much. It's true. Isn't it, Joby?" I glanced across the room at Rossannah; her head hung low staring at the floor. My heart filled with a deep longing for her.

"It's true," I conceded. "There will never be anything between the king and me." Rossannah lifted her head and we shared a tender, meaningful look.

"What's going on here?" the king appeared in the council room at my side.

"Hey," I smiled at him warmly, "What are you doing here? I thought you were going to be in the library."

"I was," he explained, "but when you didn't show up I came looking for you. We were supposed to go into the forest today. I brought my hunting gear with me."

I looked around the room at the women with varying levels of concern on their faces. They had to be overreacting. The king had never once showed any interest in any romantic involvement with me and he certainly was not "always in love" with me as the Hawk had claimed. If he had our early encounters wouldn't have been so traumatic. Besides, I think he knew somewhere within him that Rossannah and I were involved.

"Okay," I answered, "let's go." We began to leave the room, but something told me that there was one thing that I needed to do before I left. I stopped to think about what it was. The king put his hand on my shoulder and asked if I was all right. I looked at him pensively and then turned to the group of women. I walked straight over to Rossannah and put my hand on her cheek and leaned over to give her a deep, romantic kiss.

Everybody in the room gasped. I pulled away and turned to look at the king. His mouth was agape and he looked at me as if I had betrayed him. His face told me what I had needed to know. He glared at Rossannah and stalked out of the room.

CHAPTER 19

INDEPENDENCE

"You were right," I said as I sat in Rossannah's and my bedroom with Rossannah and Shyla. "You all were right. I can't believe I couldn't see it."

"You weren't looking for it," Shyla comforted me. "I saw it before anybody, except for his mother. She knew from the very beginning. She had figured it out the day that he brought you home."

"But why?" I fumed. "Why was he so…mean?"

"Only he knows that," Shyla sighed. "There is so much more I wish I knew about how your brain works, but I never will. At least everything is out in the open now, so whatever happens will happen. I just hope that there isn't too much backlash. But I know that you can fight for yourself. You've showed a lot of strength and it helps that you are in a position of power. There isn't a lot that he can do to you."

"I don't think that I'm going to have to fight," I argued. "Worst case scenario, I think we'll just go back to the way things were…not speaking."

Rossannah crawled in the bed beside me and I put my head on her shoulder. She embraced me and I felt comforted. No amount of fun could replace the feeling that I got when she held me, or I held her.

"I thought he knew about us," I told them as Rossannah stroked my hair.

"From his perspective it probably just looked like a really close friendship," Rossannah offered. "I don't know of anybody else like us."

"I wish we did," I whispered. Shyla let out a sigh and stood up to leave.

"I think I'll leave you guys alone," she said, biting her lip. I watched her go. Something told me that Shyla always wanted to say more than she thought she should.

I spent the next few days at the school with Rossannah and the Hawk. The king did not come to teach his history classes. I began to feel guilty about the way that things had happened, as if I was robbing the children of a wonderful teacher by not feeling the same way about him as he did about me. After three days he did show up again, but not for a history lesson.

"I'm going into the forest to hunt today," he explained to me, "I thought that you would like to come along. I'm sorry for reacting the way that I did. I was just shocked. I've never seen something like that before. I didn't know how to react to it."

"I think I'm going to stick around the school today," I said uneasily, "Rossannah really needs me around right now." I made sure to emphasize that I needed to stay with Rossannah. He looked hurt and walked away. I watched him through the window of the school as he made his way into the forest alone.

"Come away from the window and help me," the Hawk said as she gingerly grabbed my shoulders and lead me away from the window and into a group of children. Then she put her mouth to my ear and whispered, "don't feel guilty, you can't feel something for someone unless it's right."

I expected the Hawk to be on the side of her son, but she seemed to have her own story that would never be told and perhaps that is what contributed to her understanding of me. I looked at her sadly and she left me in the group of kids to forget my sorrows. Moments later Rossannah came to join me.

I spent the rest of the day keeping myself busy so I wouldn't have to think about the heart that I had broken. I had finally gotten to a place with the king that was uncomplicated and friendly, and it was all ruined now. I mourned the loss of his friendship, but knew that I had to be careful around him from now on.

He showed up for supper and didn't speak a word while the rest of us prattled on about the day and the things we had done. The Hawk tried to get him involved in the conversation by purposely blurting out fallacies about the history lesson she had taught that day. We all looked at him expectantly, waiting for him to correct her. He didn't seem interested in the least.

I finished first. I left the table and
Rossannah followed closely behind. We went to
our room, both exhausted from the emotionally
trying day. She left the room to go and take
a shower as I turned down the bed for when she
returned so all we had to do was crawl in and
go to sleep.

That is when I heard his footsteps behind
me. I turned around thinking that Rossannah
had forgotten something and to ask her what it
was. The king stood in front of me, looking
at me longingly and mournfully.

"Why didn't you come with me this
afternoon?" he asked, forcefully. I felt no
compulsion to lie.

"They say that you're in love with me. I
can't encourage that," I replied, stiffly.

"I see." He nodded his head. "How do you
know that you are not in love with me?"

"I'm in love with Rossannah," I answered,
quickly. "There isn't any room for anybody
else in my heart."

"Then why have you been spending the last
few weeks with me and leaving her here," he
accused, tears welling up in his eyes.

"It's never going to happen!" I shouted
angry and frustrated. "I don't have those
kinds of feeling for you. I have…sisterly
feelings for you."

He glared at me one last time, and then
walked off. I began to shake and when
Rossannah appeared in the doorway I couldn't
help but burst into tears. If I had any
doubts about his feelings they were all washed

away with his confrontation. I had hoped it was just disgust that he was feeling towards my relationship with Rossannah, but it was disappointment.

I explained what had happened to Rossannah, and she agreed to take the day off with me the next day. We went to the fields like we used to do before I began to feel the full weight of my responsibility and I got a little of my youth back with her that day. We discussed taking a trip into the forest together to visit Sheena, Cub, and Cub's children, which we hadn't done in over a year. A trip into the forest would revitalize me and I would be able to come back with renewed vigor.

We were wrenched from our daydream by Ashlee running through the golden fields toward us, waving her hands anxiously in the air trying to get our attention. When she finally reached us she had to take a moment to catch her breath before she could speak.

"He's declared war," Ashlee sputtered, "On the forest tribes. You weren't there to stop him. There wasn't any vote."

"He can't!" I screeched and began to run to the castle. I found myself standing in the council room moments later. The elderly men at the table turned to look at me. Some of them shook their heads in dismay.

"He's already left," one of them told me, sadly, "with a group of men."

"I'm going after them," I announced and ran out of the room and down the hallway. I turned a corner and bumped into Rossannah. We were both knocked to the floor from the force.

"What's going on?" Rossannah asked me. I shook my head, crying and got up. I didn't say a word as I ran off toward the stables. I heard her calling after me but didn't answer.

I swung open the door to the stables and allowed myself a second to collect myself as a painful memory slipped into my mind. I pushed it away and climbed onto the nearest horse. I forced a gush of air out of my mouth and swallowed my hatred of the beast and kicked it to force it forward. I knew that this was the only way I was going to catch up with them.

I couldn't see them in the distance. I couldn't believe that I had missed them going. I felt stupid for letting my guard down and not keeping an eye on what was going on around me. I had always been good at that.

I guided the beast through trees and ducked branches as I made the horse go as fast as I could through the forest. I could see hoof prints on the ground and I knew that they had gone this way, not even trying to hide evidence of their existence. Why would they? Everybody thought that they were at peace.

I finally caught up with them. They were resting in a clearing, ready to bed down for the night. I approached the camp cautiously and noticed that the king was nowhere to be seen. I allowed myself to be seen and ordered the men to leave and go home. They obliged me at once.

I waited in that clearing for an hour for the king to show up. He appeared carrying an armful of sticks and a pack on his back filled with game. I regretted teaching him how to survive in the forest immediately.

"Why are you doing this?" I asked him furiously. "We had an agreement. We were working for a common goal."

"We were never working for a common goal," he shouted, accusingly. "I changed for you. I tried to show you that I could understand and that we weren't so different. I can't do that anymore. There are things that I know are wrong, and I can't ignore that anymore."

"You mean Rossannah and me, don't you?" I yelled heatedly. "We are not wrong! You can't feel something for someone unless it's right!"

"Then what about me!" he sobbed. "What about what I feel for you? Isn't that wrong? Hasn't it always been wrong? You are supposed to be my enemy and I can't stop thinking about you." And then he pulled out that familiar sword. He must have gone back and finally found it after all of these years. He lifted it and charged toward me with the intention of hacking me to pieces, but his body stiffened as he reached me and his eyes searched mine in pain. He dropped the sword and slowly fell to the ground to reveal Rossannah behind him, a look of confusion and terror on her face. She had hit something with a bow and arrow for the first time.

"What do we do now?" I asked her, breathless.

"We tell the truth," Rossannah replied.

"But you will be executed!" I exclaimed.

"No," Rossannah smiled, "I won't. The people were coming after him. It seems that they don't want to have a king anymore. We are all finally free."

And from that moment on, I knew everything was going to be all right.